THEY'RE BACK...

With a sigh, I scooted on the rug until my head and shoulders were under the bed. I stretched my arm as far as it could reach, but I still couldn't touch the shoe. So I scooted even farther until only my legs were sticking out.

Then I grabbed the shoe.

I half-wiggled out from under the bed, but paused when I heard two sounds that chilled my skin. Footsteps and voices.

The footsteps were coming closer, accompanied by the murmur of voices, a man and a woman. They were walking down the hall.

And even worse!

I recognized the voices!

Eleanor Corvit and Mitch Crouch had returned.

Don't miss the first book in the series:
ReGeneration

ReGeneration

The Search

L. J. Singleton

BERKLEY JAM BOOKS, NEW YORK

REGENERATION: THE SEARCH

A Berkley Jam Book / published by arrangement with the author

PRINTING HISTORY
Berkley Jam edition / March 2000

The Penguin Putnam Inc. World Wide Web site address is
http://www.penguinputnam.com

ISBN: 0-425-17368-2

BERKLEY JAM BOOKS®
Berkley Jam Books are published by The Berkley Publishing Group,
a division of Penguin Putnam Inc.,
375 Hudson Street, New York, New York 10014.
BERKLEY JAM and its logo
are trademarks belonging to Penguin Putnam Inc.

PRINTED IN THE UNITED STATES OF AMERICA

10 9 8 7 6 5 4 3 2 1

With special thanks
to my good friends in Texas:
Melody DeLeon and her daughters,
Alicia, Lucia, and Rachel.

ReGeneration

The Search

ONE

"RUN!" I shouted. "RENEGADE! GET OUT OF THE ROAD!"

But the yellow Lab pup sitting about a mile from me couldn't hear my warning.

And when I peered in the other direction, my special sight stretching another mile down the road, my stomach twisted with terror.

The pale gray car was still coming.

FAST.

Shoving my thick-lensed glasses into one pocket of my hunting jacket and my tape recorder in the other, I raced toward the distant road. I'd never make it in time.

Never.

Without the glasses to steady the ground and clarify obstacles, my eyes watered. I rubbed them, feeling the usual sense of dizziness as I struggled to adjust my vision. I was nearly at the end of the pasture, where dense woods bordered the ranch. My brothers and I used to have a fort called Boys Rule in these woods, so I knew them well. But if my legs didn't carry me fast enough, that wouldn't matter much.

Spindly branches and overwhelming greenness seemed to suck me in, blurring my perception of light and dark, near and far. I could see great when I wore my glasses, but without them distant shapes came closer, and closer shapes distorted.

Testing my unusual vision was the reason I'd been in the pasture at the edge of the woods. Recording extraordinary measurements in my mini–tape recorder, I'd been amazed to view tiny multilegged insects on a far-off stump. I'd looked even farther, a mile away to the blacktop oil road where the runt six-month-old pup lazed in the noon sun.

But then I'd spotted the swift-moving car.

"RENEGADE!" I called out again, stumbling into a bush, falling, but then picking myself up. Klutz. That's what they called me, kids who razzed me at school and even my brothers Larry Joe and Marcos when we were going at it. They were right.

I used to laugh at my klutziness. Sometimes I'd put on outrageous wigs and paint my dark skin bright colors, then twist colorful balloons into wacky animals or wild hats. Playing the family clown made me feel special— like I was doing something good. But then I'd learned the reason for my awkwardness. Allison, Varina, and Chase had traveled all the way from California to tell me the incredible truth.

I was a clone.

C-L-O-N-E. Not an abandoned baby, but an abandoned experiment. I'd been created in a floating lab on a yacht, designed for study and examination. Eric Prince: a genetic specimen.

The ground dipped and I fell hard, this time into a dried creek bed, and my knee stung where the cloth ripped away in a jagged tear. But it was nothing compared with what would happen if I couldn't reach the road before the speeding car turned the final corner.

As I zoomed my gaze beyond dense trees, seeing through branches and brambles to the seemingly quiet country road less than a hundred yards away, my heart thumped even faster.

Renegade was a bull's-eye target. Curled up in the center of the road, he nipped at some fleas, enjoying a brief spell of sunshine. The pup lifted his yellow head lazily, glanced around, then resumed flea-nipping.

And the speeding car continued forward, wheels spinning, churning, roaring toward Renegade.

"Hurry!" I told myself, willing my thin legs to leap long and far, and praying I wouldn't fall again. Closer now and yet still too far to warn the wayward pup. I called to Renegade over and over again, but knew he couldn't hear. The canine target was helpless in the path of death, with only one hope: me.

Who asked to be a clone, anyway? My powerful vision was a gift, yes, but it was also a curse. And I cursed this gift that showed me danger and yet hampered the simple act of running.

Frustrated, I reached for my glasses. When I put them on the near world came into view, but I could no longer see far away. With the glasses, it was as if the road, the car, and Renegade had vanished from sight.

But a frightening sound came closer. A roaring motor, winding faster than the limit on the rural oil road. The car didn't belong to a neighbor or friend. Strangers, I'd already guessed from the rental-car sticker on the license plate.

It shocked me to realize that I'd actually been able to see a license plate maybe two miles away! I forced myself to speed up—around trees, over rough ground, and through prickly bushes. Pounding feet, thumping heart, sweaty brow, and clenched hands. I ran as if my life depended on it—because Renegade's did.

Just a little farther and the woods would unfold into a seldom-used ribbon of road. The motor roared louder . . . closer, but still invisible through the trees. My ears sharpened and I heard the squeal of wheels tilting at the sharp hairpin turn: the final corner.

A whine of brakes screamed a warning; sharp honks, the hot smell of burnt rubber, a startled bark . . . and then nothing.

With tears streaming from my cursed eyes, I kept running . . . until I finally reached the road.

TWO

Renegade was lying in a ditch.
Unmoving.

Still as death.

"Oh, no!" I sobbed, blaming myself for having super eyesight and not super speed. What was the point in being a clone if I couldn't help others? On my computer games when I gained powers I could conquer impossible obstacles. But even with my awesome eyesight, I was still Eric the Klutz.

The car had continued on, its rumble fading in the distance. I bent down beside the dog. Reaching out, I hesitated, then gently touched the silky yellow fur. Still warm. So peaceful, so soft, as if he were sleeping. Amazingly, there were no obvious injuries: no blood, bashed bones, or oily treadmarks.

Suddenly Renegade's long red tongue poked out and slurped a happy kiss on my hand.

"Renegade!" I jumped, astonished. "You're all right!"

The dog answered with a yip, wagging his tail and scrambling upright on all four legs.

"WOW! I can't believe it! The car didn't touch a hair on your hide, you scamp." I wrapped my arms around the dog and squeezed hard. "Bet you jumped out of the way and just had the wind knocked out of you."

Renegade slurped another doggy kiss and whined with joy. I could hardly let the pup go, I was so relieved.

Wait till I told my parents about that irresponsible driver! It was fortunate I'd seen the license plate. To make sure I reported it right, I reached into my pocket and withdrew my tape recorder. Then I repeated the gray car's license number, remembering to add that it was a rented car.

"I knew they weren't from around here," I muttered, feeling a wave of anger at anyone who could knock a dog into a ditch and not even stop to check and see if he was okay.

I wondered who'd been driving the car. I'd glimpsed a man at the wheel and a woman beside him. Where were they headed? There were only a few ranches on this rural road: my family, the Hees, and the DeLeons. I hadn't heard of anyone having out-of-town company.

"Come on, Renegade. Let's head back home," I said, looking carefully both ways as I crossed the road with the pup loping beside me.

I walked quickly, surefooted, having no trouble with blurred weeds and ruts in the ground thanks to my glasses. Still, the urge to take the glasses off and continue on with more experiments was strong. My irregular eyesight, which I'd always thought was a handicap, was superhuman. The kind of stuff I'd read about in comic books but never expected to actually experience.

My parents and the other clones had warned me to keep it a secret, but I was bursting to tell Marcos and Larry Joe. They'd be totally blown away. And they'd never call me a four-eyed geek again.

Grinning, I imagined showing off my super vision. Marcos was younger than me, but when he and Larry Joe got together, I felt like *I* was the "little" brother. Larry Joe thought he knew everything and could do anything just because he was older and had such strong muscles from pushing his wheelchair. I didn't need a wheelchair, but to be fair I used one when I played basketball against my brothers. I couldn't maneuver or spin as skillfully as they could, so they always whopped me big-time. But I had fun, and I was used to losing.

I slowed as I reached the fence that surrounded the pasture. I paused to open the livestock gate, then slipped through it. Up ahead, I could see our red barn and beyond that the roof of our rambling green-and-white ranch home.

I started walking faster, until I was running toward my house. Renegade thought this was a fun game, and barked playfully beside me.

"Okay, boy," I said with forced enthusiasm. "Let's race!"

The dog barked again, sniffing the air and leaping up, excited to be headed home. I understood how he felt. Home was safe. A place where you could count on family.

And I had PLENTY of family. There were ten of us Prince kids. Six boys and four girls, all adoptees, ages two to seventeen, with mixed heritages and challenges. It was a hoot when a new kid came to school and met one of us, then another, another, and so on. . . .

Varina, Chase, and Allison had been surprised by my

large family. They were all only children and didn't understand the bonds of a big family. They'd expected me to leave my home and join them in California because of what we had in common. Of course, my parents refused. We Princes tend to stick together, good or bad. And that's the way we like it.

Renegade bounded along happily beside me, perking his ears at the sound of someone bouncing a ball at the hoop-court by the front driveway. The dog glanced at me as if asking permission to run ahead. When I nodded, he barked and disappeared around the corner.

Seconds later, I heard him bark again. But this time the sound was deep and suspicious.

I picked up my pace, passing the garden, hurrying past garbage cans and beyond the raised porch.

As I reached the front yard, I stopped in shock. I stared at the car parked in the driveway.

A gray sedan with Dallas plates.

The reckless driver.

At MY house.

THREE

There was no one in the car, but I couldn't stop staring. What in the world was it doing here?

"Hey, Klutz!" I heard a voice call from the basketball court. "Eric, where ya been all morning?"

I glanced at dark-haired, broad-shouldered Larry Joe, who twirled the ball on his fingertip with one hand and rolled his wheelchair expertly with his other.

"Who's that car belong to?" I asked tensely.

"Don't know," Larry Joe said with a shrug. "Wanna shoot some hoops?"

"No. I want to know about that car."

"I didn't see nothing. Go inside and ask Mom. Probably some of her quilting club friends."

"I doubt it. None of Mom's friends would rent a car in Dallas. You sure you didn't see anything?"

"He didn't, but I did," a shrill voice piped up. I turned and saw my sister Kristyn. I usually took off before she could bug me. Just my luck The Pain would have the answers. Kristyn was fifteen like me, and always following me around, copying EVERYTHING I did. Last month, she'd actually gotten a tattoo on her ankle similar to the one I'd had since birth. If I'd pulled a stunt like that, I'd have been grounded for life. But Kristyn was grounded for a mere week. Mom and Dad were always soft with her, maybe because Kristyn's leukemia had only been in remission for a year and they were afraid it would come back.

"It was an old lady and a young guy," Kristyn said, her almond-shaped black eyes sparkling with pride. "They're in the house talking to Mom and Dad. And get this—they're from New York!"

"You're making that up," I accused.

"New York?" Even Larry Joe looked surprised. "No fooling?"

"It's the truth," Kristyn insisted. "I was emptying the dishwasher when they came into the house, and I heard them say they were from a TV show."

"WOW!" Larry Joe exclaimed. "I always wanted to be on TV. Maybe they could introduce me to some famous basketball players. Wouldn't that be cool, Eric?"

I nodded, but felt uneasy.

"This is SO exciting." Kristyn practically danced in the driveway. "Almost as exciting as my being on the float tonight at the Christmas Parade. Hey, maybe that's why they're here. To film ME! I'm going back inside to hear more."

"I'd better find out more, too," I murmured.

The three of us headed up the ramp onto the front porch, and then into the house. Kristyn and Larry Joe kidded around about riches, fame, and celebrities, but I walked with the solemnity of a visit to the principal's office. Publicity could be dangerous.

I felt a nudge on my leg, looked down, and saw that Renegade had followed me. His tail wagged and he took off eagerly for the living room. I heard a man laugh and say, "What a great-looking dog."

Could it be the same man who'd been driving the gray car and nearly killed Renegade only a short time ago?

"Let's go meet the visitors," Kristyn said, tugging on my hand.

"Not me." I pulled away. "I'll wait by the kitchen."

"I'll go with you," Larry Joe told Kristyn. "Wonder if they know any basketball stars."

"Or fashion models," Kristyn added, lifting her head and fluffing her long silky black hair. She was part Asian, with golden skin, and people were always saying she could be a model. She was skinny enough, and tall, too—three inches taller than me, which was downright embarrassing.

After Kristyn and Larry Joe left, I crept closer to the living room, leaning against the wall and peeking inside.

Kristyn was giggling and shaking hands with a chubby gray-haired, well-dressed woman. Larry Joe grinned and said "Howdoyoudo" to the twenty-something guy with a reddish mustache. And my parents sat side by side on the couch, smiling and leaning forward with interest.

"What lovely children!" the elderly woman gushed. "I'm delighted to meet you. I'm Eleanor Corvit and this is my photographer, Mitch Crouch."

"Do you ever take pictures of famous hoop stars, Mr. Crouch?" Larry Joe asked eagerly.

"Sure, kid." He idly stroked his mustache. "You like to play basketball?"

"You betcha." Larry Joe's grin practically filled the room. "Come outside and I'll show you."

Dad shook his head. "Not right now. We haven't finished business yet."

Business? I learned closer. Exactly WHAT kind of business?

My curiosity mingled with quick anger. How could these strangers sit calmly in our living room after what they'd almost done to Renegade? Not that Renegade held a grudge. He sat at their feet, his tail tapping out a contented welcome. I wondered what would happen if I told my parents our visitors had nearly killed Renegade.

But I stayed back and held my tongue.

I studied Eleanor Corvit, who reminded me of my grandma Millie, except for her fancy, designer-type clothes. She seemed classy and cozy, not the kind of person who'd hit-and-run a defenseless dog. But then Mitch had been driving, and he was strumming his fingers against his chair in an intense, impatient way.

"As I've explained, we've chosen you for a profile on exceptional families," Eleanor Corvit said to my parents.

Kristyn frowned. "So you're not here because of tonight's parade?"

"A parade at night?" Mitch questioned. "Won't it be too dark?"

"It's a light parade, and the largest holiday parade in the whole country," Mom replied proudly. "There'll be over one hundred floats, bands, and walking units."

"And I'm going to be on a float," Kristyn added proudly. "In an angel costume with huge glowing wings."

"Wonderful!" Eleanor beamed. "We'll have to come to watch. But right now we'd like to interview your lovely family."

"For TV?" Dad asked with a frown. And when Eleanor nodded, he shook his head. "I don't know. We're not TV-type folks."

"Give it a chance, dear. It could be fun," Mom said with a wink at Larry Joe and Kristyn. "I know the kids would love it."

Not me, I thought with a frown. And I knew Allison, Varina, and Chase would agree. They'd warned me about the dangerous people who knew about the clone experiment and wanted to study us—or worse. So I had to be careful, guard my secrets, and keep a low profile. Appearing on TV was a BAD idea.

But Mom's face was lit up like the Christmas Parade. "I'd love to do the show," she said. "Only the kids will have to decide for themselves."

"I vote YES!" Kristyn cried.

"Me too!" Larry Joe added.

"Pipe down so we can hear the details." Dad turned back to the strangers. "What did you say your show was called?"

"*Real Families*. It's a VERY popular cable show," Eleanor said, patting her gray curls. "We do segments on ordinary people living extraordinary lives. By appearing on our show, you'll encourage more people to adopt special-needs children. Are all of your children adopted?"

"Oh, yes," Mom answered. "It's always been our dream to have a large family. We've been blessed with wonderful kids."

"Like me," Larry Joe piped up. Nothing modest about him.

Dad chuckled. "You're all terrific. But you and Kristyn skedaddle so we can have a quiet talk."

"I'm being quiet," Kristyn said with a pout. "Can't I stay?"

"Krissy, you are NEVER quiet." Mom reached out to smooth Kristyn's silky hair. "Besides, you need to finish emptying the dishwasher, then get ready for tonight."

Watching, I couldn't help but grin. Kristyn's pouty act didn't work this time. Served The Pain right.

"I'd prefer the children stay," Eleanor interjected. "In fact, I'd like to do some interviews today."

Dad folded his arms. "If the kids want to be interviewed, it's their choice."

"Of course. But I'm sure there will be no problems," Eleanor said, her tone as sweet as powdered sugar sprinkled on warm cookies. "I'll begin by interviewing the older children first."

"Yesss! I'm the oldest," Larry Joe exclaimed.

"And I'm third oldest," Kristyn added.

"Wonderful!" Eleanor smoothed out a crease in her long paisley skirt. "I can't wait to get to know each one of you. But I want to do it in a fair, orderly manner, starting with three interviews today."

"Fine with me," Mom said with a nod. Dad just gave a low grunt; he clearly wasn't convinced, but didn't want to upset Mom.

Eleanor glanced around. "Is the second-oldest child at home?"

"Eric sure is." Larry Joe snickered with a glance at the doorway where I crouched.

"Splendid," Eleanor said. "First I'll talk to you, Larry Joe. And then next, I'll interview Eric."

FOUR

'm out of here! I thought.

I jumped up and tore around the kitchen, down the hall, and into the bedroom I shared with Larry Joe and Marcos.

Eleanor Corvit seemed like a sweet old lady, but I didn't trust that Mitch. Anyone who'd nearly hit a dog and then just drive away was sewer-scum.

My name was being called, but I didn't answer. Instead, I ducked into the closet, pushing aside clothes and school backpacks, then hiding behind a heavy winter jacket. I didn't move a fraction, standing still and silent. I heard the bedroom door open, Kristyn say, "He's not here," and then the door shut.

"Whew! That was close," I murmured, smoothing my hair back in place as I went over to my computer. I powered up and accessed the World Wide Web. Whenever in doubt, look for the facts. So I found a search engine and typed in *"Real Families."*

The computer hummed with purpose and showed over twenty matches. After I read a few, my worries eased a bit. *Real Families* was a popular, respected show. It highlighted families who volunteered in homeless shelters, did animal rescues, and ran in marathons.

Now it wanted to interview MY family.

My suspicions faded and gave way to pride. My family WAS special. Mom and Dad were great and deserved to be honored on a TV show.

I felt foolish for running off and hiding. A major overreaction. I mean, a month ago I would have been thrilled to be on TV. But finding out I'd been created from an experiment had changed me. Since then, I'd been looking over my shoulder, afraid someone would come after me like they had the other clones.

Chase, Allison, and Varina.

I sighed, wondering how they were doing. I'd had one short letter from Allison, but no other news.

I powered down my computer and shut it off. Then I reached into the bottom of my sock drawer, pulled out Allison's letter, and read the strong, energetic handwriting.

Hey, Eric!

How's it going? All the excitement's over and the bad dudes are gone. Varina's uncle is out of the hospital. They hired a nurse, so they didn't need me hanging around. That's why I'm back living at my prissy princess school. Bor-ring!

I had hoped us C.C.'s would be like a family, but I guess it's not gonna happen. Safer to stay

apart. Still, if you need anything, call me. Okay?
Your C.C. . . . Allison

   P.S. Chase left to find Sandee.

I knew the letter by heart! But instead of offering answers, it only raised more questions. Like what had happened to "bad dude" Dr. Mansfield Victor after he tried to kill Varina? I'd searched on the Internet and found a small news article about the attack and subsequent arrest, but then nothing. And what about Dr. Victor's wife, Geneva? Had she been arrested, too?

I also wondered about Varina's uncle Jim—one of the doctors who'd created us clones fifteen years ago. After a vicious assault (probably by Dr. Victor), Dr. Jim Fergus had lapsed into a coma. He was out of the hospital, but was he well enough to tell Varina more about the clone experiment? Or had Varina, with her super memory, remembered important facts about the past on her own?

Of course, the biggest mystery concerned the missing clone. Where was Sandee Yoon? Chase and Allison had flown to Colorado in search of Sandee, only to learn she was a runaway. And now Chase was on Sandee's trail. But would he be able to find her?

I'd written back to Allison, asking these and more questions, only she hadn't replied yet. So I was left waiting.

Tired of waiting for an answer, I'd started doing tests on my unusual eyesight. The measurements were incredible. And each time I tested, my vision zoomed farther.

I wanted to share these findings with Allison, but there'd never been a good enough reason to call her.

Until now.

Glancing at my watch, I guessed it would be almost noon in San Francisco. Allison was probably out volunteering for Habitat for Humanity. Her clone power was super strength, and she thrived on hard physical work. Allison was the kind of person who'd get a kick out of wacky wigs and balloon animals, a dedicated do-gooder with the enthusiasm of a cheerleader. I'd liked her right away.

It was Allison who'd said we clones were like a family. And she'd called us C.C.'s: Clone Cousins.

Right now I sure could have used some cousinly advice.

I jotted down Allison's number on a scrap of paper, carefully put her letter away, then crept out of my room to use the phone.

I heard the low murmur of conversation from the living room. The visitors were still here. But at least no one was calling my name anymore. Hopefully they'd decided to interview Kristyn or Marcos instead.

Lifting the receiver, I punched in Allison's phone number.

I held my breath . . . waiting. . . .

One ring. Two. Four . . . and then I heard Allison's voice.

"Hey! Sorry, but I'm unable to come to the phone right now. If you'd care to leave your name, a short message . . ."

I stopped listening, and tightened my fist.

Think quick, Eric. Do you want to leave a message? Is it safe for Allison to call back? What if someone overhears? I didn't want to put Allison in danger.

So I hung up.

Disappointed, I slowly turned around—only to find myself staring at The Pain.

"I found him!" Kristyn shouted out to anyone within a mile's radius. She grabbed my arm and yanked me forward. "Where have you been, Eric? We've been looking all over for you."

"I—I . . . uh . . ." I couldn't think of anything I wanted to say, so I just shrugged.

"Well, come on!" Kristyn's dark eyes sparkled. "Our guests just interviewed me and it was SO thrilling. But now it's your turn. Hurry, Eric! They want to talk to you!"

FIVE

Los Angeles, CA

"I want to talk with him," the girl with blond-streaked short, dark hair insisted, her black eyes shining with determination.

"Lighten up, Serena." Amishka sounded bored as she adjusted her wig. "Just help me get ready for tonight. Hey, can I borrow your ankle bracelet? That silver dolphin design is SO wicked."

"No one wears my ankle band except me. Besides, you're changing the subject. I'm talking about MY life here. Come on, Amishka, make this happen for me. PLEASE!"

"No dice." Amishka reached for her makeup case. "Just finish sewing my red-beaded skirt. You're my assistant, not a voice. Got it?"

"Oh, I got it, all right. All the way up to your nose

ring," Serena spat out. Then, with a furious sound, she tossed the red-beaded skirt on the floor and stomped out of the hotel room.

Serena's anger bubbled beyond the boiling point. For nearly a year, she'd been Amishka's slave, and for WHAT? A few bucks here and there, a place to crash at night, but not what she'd been promised. When was Serena going to get her chance on the stage? She could sing better than anyone in the group. If Slam, the Fever Pitch's lead singer, would just listen. . . .

Amishka kept promising to put in a good word with Slam, but months passed and nothing changed. Serena was dirt-tired of being Amishka's lapdog. Fetch this, fix that, roll over, and stay out of my way.

Fine! Serena thought. I'll stay out of your way big-time. I'm out of here! But first I'm gonna make Slam listen.

She stormed down the hall, punching the elevator to the 17th floor. Since Fever Pitch was only an opening act, it didn't rate the Penthouse. That honor went to the BNT (Big Name Talent), the infamous bad-boy rocker, Ravage. Serena still couldn't believe she was staying in the same hotel as superstar Ravage. She'd die for his autograph, or just to see him up close. . . . WOW!

All her life she'd only had one ambition: to be the next Brandy or Britney Spears. Her friends raved about her singing, and they weren't just being nice. Her voice was exceptional. She could actually shatter glass when she hit high notes—a REAL rush.

But she wouldn't get anywhere in Colorado. So she'd dumped her totally dysfunctional family, changed her name and her appearance, then headed for sunny, smoggy Los Angeles. She'd figured it'd only be a matter of time before she hit wealth, fame, and superstardom.

Well, time's up, she thought, her fury fueling her to take action. No more waiting till Amishka said the time was right.

I'll make now right.

Reaching the 17th floor, she headed for the suite of rooms belonging to Slam. As she neared the rooms, she saw Slam entering a side door marked "To Stairwell."

"Slam!" she called, only he'd already disappeared through the door. So Serena followed.

She paused as the door shut, and listened. Above her she heard light, quick footsteps. Where was Slam going? Not the Penthouse, she realized, when she passed a door leading to the prestigious top floor. But what was higher than the Penthouse?

Seconds later she found out when she reached a door marked "Roof." Puzzled, she pushed it open.

Slam wasn't in sight, but she could still hear the hurried sounds of his footsteps. Before shutting the door, she checked the knob to make sure it wouldn't lock behind her. She had a phobia of water, not heights. Still, she didn't want to be trapped up here. Fortunately the knob didn't automatically lock. So she continued after Slam.

Who'd have thought a roof could be so BIG? And it wasn't flat like she'd imagined, either. A huge humming air-conditioning unit and other bulky outcroppings created a maze.

Serena still had enough anger to keep her going. She WAS going to find Slam. He WAS going to listen to her. And she WAS going to be a star.

But finding Slam wasn't so easy. By the time she'd made it around the air conditioner and stood by the front edge of the roof, she was alone.

"Slam?" she called out at the same time she heard a

door shut behind her. Following the sound, she squeezed through a narrow passage between two walls, and saw another door.

When she reached for the knob, it was locked.

She wiggled and tugged on the knob, but it wouldn't give. Swearing, she kicked the door. "I missed him!"

She swore some more, then looked around, and tried to figure out which way to go. Probably back the way she came. At least she knew that door wasn't locked.

But when she squeezed through the narrow passage again, she found herself at the back of the roof, not the front. A wide open area sprawled out before her and she noticed painted markings on the cement, perhaps a helicopter landing.

And that wasn't all she noticed.

She choked back a gasp and just stared.

NO WAY! She had to be seeing things.

So she closed her eyes and shook her head as if her vision was an Etch-A-Sketch that could be jiggled clear. Then she opened her eyes again.

But the THING was still there.

A long, curved dark wood box.

A coffin.

SIX

Eleanor Corvit invited me to sit on the couch beside her, and she sounded so sweet and grandmotherly I couldn't refuse.

"Yes, ma'am," I said, suddenly feeling shy. My siblings and parents had left the room, so I was alone with our visitors. It didn't help that maniac-driver Mitch stood nearby holding a camera. He watched me like a buzzard eyeing fresh roadkill.

"I want to hear all about you, Eric," Eleanor said warmly.

"Ain't much to say, ma'am." I shrugged, squirming under the Buzzard's intense gaze.

"You Prince children are so polite," she said with a chuckle. "Your parents have done a wonderful job raising you, and I'm delighted to be here. Now we'll get to know each other. So sit back and relax."

"I'll try."

"Tell us about yourself."

"Begging your pardon, ma'am." I gulped and decided I couldn't sit here and ignore what I was really thinking.

"Yes?"

"Before we talk, there's something you should tell my parents." I glanced to where Renegade curled in a trusting ball at my feet.

"What do you mean?" Eleanor tilted her head, clearly puzzled. But Mitch scowled and looked away, guilty-like.

"Earlier, I saw your car. Going really fast." I didn't add how far away I was at the time.

"You did?" Eleanor's eyes widened. "Then you must know how upsetting it was. I didn't think I'd ever stop shaking."

"You? Shaking?" Had I missed something here? "But you nearly killed Renegade. And you didn't even stop."

"That was my fault," Mitch confessed, his shoulders slumped and his expression remorseful. "Eleanor has a bad heart and I was afraid to upset her."

"I told you to turn around and check on that poor creature," Eleanor said, her frail voice cracking with emotion.

"But I thought it was a wolf," Mitch argued. Then he turned to me with a sigh. "All I saw was a quick blur of tan. It wasn't until I met this dog, I realized what had happened. Or ALMOST happened. I'm glad your dog is all right."

"Me too."

Mitch grinned and reached out to pat Renegade. "Good thing you move fast, fella. I'd hate to hurt a great dog like you."

"He IS really great," I said, relaxing into a smile. I'd

have to learn not to jump to conclusions so quickly. Mitch was an okay guy after all.

"Eric dear, let's talk about YOU." The wrinkles around Eleanor's mouth deepened with her smile.

"Sure."

"Start at the beginning. Such as, how old were you when you were adopted?"

I started to say almost two years old, but then stopped myself. If I told the truth on TV, someone watching might realize I was a clone. That could put the other clones and my own family in danger.

So I lied, "I was a few hours old when I was adopted."

"Do you know anything about your biological family?" Eleanor asked, jotting notes in a leather-bound book.

"Yeah." I glanced at the camera on Mitch's lap and pretended I was being interviewed live, and that somewhere out there in TV land, wicked Dr. Victor and Geneva were watching.

"Tell us about your birth parents," Eleanor prompted.

"My real mother was only a teenager when I was born, but since she went to college instead of raising me, she's a doctor now."

"How nice," Eleanor said, smiling. "And your birth father?"

"Well, uh, he's a magician. He travels with a circus and sends me postcards from all over the world."

"How fascinating! I'd love to interview him, too." Eleanor took more notes, and my stomach churned. Maybe I'd lied a bit too well. What if they investigated my "father" and found out he didn't exist? I decided I'd better stick to the truth for the rest of the interview.

But before Eleanor could ask me any more questions, Mitch arched his brows at her, a silent message of some kind. Had they guessed I was lying? Something must have happened, because suddenly Eleanor stood up.

"It's been lovely chatting with you, Eric." Eleanor patted her gray curls.

"You're done with me?" I asked, relieved and surprised.

"Yes." She glanced over at Mitch. "We've taken enough of your family's time today. You've all been so helpful."

I glanced away, knowing how little help I'd been.

Mitch pushed back his reddish-brown hair. "See you later, Eric."

"Yeah. Maybe at the parade tonight. Will you be there?"

"You can count on us. We wouldn't miss watching your lovely sister on her float. Tell your parents I'll be in touch," Eleanor said as she picked up her purse.

And then they were gone. But minutes later, I discovered they'd left something behind.

held Mitch's camera carefully, afraid I might drop or damage it. I'd heard that photographers were really protective over their cameras. And yet Mitch had forgotten his. I figured he'd probably freak when he realized his camera was missing, and hoped my parents had his phone number so we could let him know it was safe.

Or better yet, I'd return the camera personally. Yeah, good idea. Then maybe I'd stop feeling so guilty about lying.

Eleanor Corvit and Mitch Crouch had mentioned staying in town, so they were probably at one of the elegant bed-and-breakfast inns. It shouldn't be too hard to find them, I thought.

All I had to do was get a ride into town. But even that proved easy. When I told my parents about the camera, they said I could tag along when they dropped Kristyn off. Since she was going to be in the parade, she

needed to arrive a few hours early for practice and prep-
aration.

The sun was low in the sky by the time we left Kristyn
at her school. Then my parents drove me to the largest
and most luxurious B&B in town, the Bloomtree Inn.

"When you're done returning the camera, go to the
bleachers and wait for us," Mom told me through the
open car window. "We'll be back in an hour to get good
spots for the parade."

"Yes, ma'am." I reached over and kissed Mom's
cheek, then waved at Dad behind the driver's seat. Turning away, I headed for the sprawling multistoried inn.

Bloomtree Inn was bustling, filled with parade enthusiasm. After waiting in line at the front desk, I talked to
a clerk named Virginia (who just happened to be the
sister of one of my teachers). Virginia checked a computer and discovered there were no guests under the
name Corvit or Crouch. But she made a few calls and
found out a Mrs. E. Corvit was registered at the Willows
Bed and Breakfast Inn.

Yes! After thanking Virginia, I hurried to the Willows
Inn, which was only a few blocks away.

This inn was a refurbished Victorian house, tall and
rambling, painted pale yellow and off-white, with cool
arches and stained-glass windows. I'd never been inside,
although I'd been driven past a million times.

Tucking my T-shirt into my jeans and trying to look
presentable, I walked up the wrought iron–laced entry-
way and stepped into a warm, old-fashioned parlor. An-
tique lamps were turned low, setting the mood of a
long-ago era. And a few guests sat in a quiet corner,
sipping tea and speaking softly.

I walked toward a large dark-haired woman carrying
towels. "Excuse me, uh, I'm looking for Mrs. Corvit."

When she turned, I recognized her from church, although I couldn't recall her name.

Pushing up her wire-frame glasses, the woman peered down at me. "I know you. You're one of the Prince boys."

"Yes, ma'am. I'm Eric." I shifted my feet and stared down at my scuffed and dirty sneakers. "I'm looking for Mrs. Corvit or her friend Mr. Crouch."

"Our New York guests." She grinned. "They're staying in the Violet and Turquoise Rooms. Only they're not here now."

"They aren't?" I asked, dismayed.

"No. I saw them drive in a while ago, but then they left again. I'm supposing they went out for a bite to eat."

"Darn." I held out the paper bag that held the camera. "I wanted to return Mr. Crouch's camera. He left it out at our place."

"They were way out at your place?" Her ears perked, clearly eager for gossip. "Are they friends of the family?"

"Sort of. I just want to return the camera."

"Their rooms are at the end of the hall. You caught me as I was putting fresh towels in, so the door's open. Go on and leave the camera. I'm sure your friends won't mind."

"Thank you, ma'am." Then before she could ask any more questions, I turned and hurried down the hall.

I found the open door labeled "Violet Room" and glanced uncertainly inside. The ornate frame bed was made neatly, the patchwork quilt decorated with crocheted-lace pillows. There were several very expensive-looking leather suitcases on the floor and I glimpsed women's suits hung in the wardrobe case. This had to be Mrs. Corvit's room.

Taking a step inside the room, I walked over to the bed and set the bag down. Then I turned around to leave, but my clumsy foot bumped into one of the leather suitcases, knocking it into the other suitcases, causing all three of them to tilt, teeter, and topple to the floor like dominos.

"Oh, no!" I cried when I saw that one of the suitcases had popped open, spilling out a treasure trove of ladies' shoes.

High-heeled shoes, shiny red flats, silver shoes with pointy toes, purple sandals, running shoes, suede slippers. I'd never seen so many shoes in my life!

I began to carefully place the shoes back into the suitcase. I counted the shoes—thirteen pairs! All for ONE set of feet? Was that possible?

I had just closed the suitcase when a flash of silver under the bed caught my eye. Bending low, I saw that one silver shoe had tumbled out of reach. Darn! I'd have to crawl under the bed.

With a sigh, I scooted on the rug until my head and shoulders were under the bed. I stretched my arm as far as it could reach, but I still couldn't touch the shoe. So I scooted even farther until only my legs were sticking out.

Then I grabbed the shoe.

YES! SUCCESS!!

A bright red price tag was still affixed to the bottom of the shoe. Curious, I checked it out and then gave a low whistle at the price. I could have bought four or five new computer games for that much! Even the shoe store's name sounded expensive—Pacific Soles.

I half-wiggled out from under the bed, but paused when I heard two sounds that chilled my skin. Footsteps and voices.

The footsteps were coming closer, accompanied by the murmur of voices, a man and a woman. They were walking down the hall.

And even worse!

I recognized the voices.

Eleanor Corvit and Mitch Crouch had returned.

EIGHT

I had two choices. Number one. Be caught lurking under the bed with a lady's shoe in my hand. Or number two. Hide.

My parents didn't raise a dummy. I chose to hide.

Only when I scooted quickly and tucked my legs to my chest, I bumped my face against the bed frame . . . and my glasses fell off.

Could there be a worse klutz in the entire universe?

Thoroughly disgusted with myself, I lay there in a scrunched-up ball, afraid to move or breathe. I remembered Mrs. Corvit saying she planned on going to the parade, so I shouldn't be stuck in here for too long, I reasoned.

At least, I hoped not.

"Mitch, let's make this quick," Mrs. Corvit said, sitting on the edge of the bed, which caused the mattress springs to bounce and tickle me.

"Sure. No reason to stick around now."

"Thank goodness we were able to learn what we needed in only three interviews. I feel like I've been away from civilization for years," she said, her leather half-boots only inches from my nose, although with my vision starting to blur it was hard to see clearly.

"Hey, I grew up in a small town. Not a lot of action, but I kind of like the slower pace."

"That doesn't surprise me considering YOUR history," Mrs. Corvit said with an edge to her voice that startled me. What had happened to the grandmotherly sweetness?

"You hired me 'cause of my history," he retorted, sounding equally nasty. "Don't forget that."

"I haven't forgotten anything, nor do I intend to. You've done a good job so far, so don't tick me off now. Let's just collect our things and check out."

"Yeah, the faster the better. Although I hate to miss the light parade. Would have been fun."

"Only if you want to risk another stint in prison." The springs above me jiggled again and I heard the shuffling of a paper bag. "Mitch, what is THIS? How did YOUR camera get on MY bed?"

"Dunno. I thought I left it at the Prince house."

"You DID, which was incredibly careless. I warned you against drawing attention to yourself," she snarled.

"Hey, we got the camera back. So no harm done."

Through my blurry vision, I saw dark brown shoes moving close to the leather boots. My whole body was quaking and I couldn't believe what I was hearing. Mitch had been in prison? Was that why Mrs. Corvit sounded so unfriendly? And why weren't they staying for the parade? They hadn't finished interviewing my family yet.

Suddenly something dark and fuzzy plopped onto the floor. I almost cried out, thinking it was some kind of dead animal. But I forced my eyes to focus and I realized it was just a wig. A gray wig.

"That feels SO much better," I heard Mrs. Corvit say with a soft voice that suddenly sounded much younger.

What was going on? Why would she wear a wig? The only time I'd known anyone to wear one was when Kristyn's hair fell out after chemo a few years ago. So either Mrs. Corvit had worse health than the heart problem Mitch had mentioned earlier or else she was a fake.

My suspicions grew, new fears filling me.

I heard Mitch leave, probably heading to his own room. I tensed as Mrs. Corvit opened a suitcase and coat hangers rattled as she finished packing. She hummed a cheery tune while she worked, as though she was in a great mood. I only hoped she didn't check her shoes and realize one was missing. If she started looking for it and found me hiding under her bed, her good mood would end in a hurry.

I hadn't been discovered by the time Mitch returned with his suitcase—at least I think the bulky dark shape was a suitcase. It was hard to see up close without my glasses. Other shapes kept crowding into view; dark gray, blue, and brown clothing—as if I was seeing IN-SIDE the suitcase.

Startled, I jerked my head away, afraid to look deeper.

"What was that?" Mrs. Corvit suddenly asked.

I froze, shut my eyes, and held myself so still I could have been a statue.

"What was WHAT?" Mitch asked, impatiently.

"I heard a sound. At least, I think I did. Check the door and window, just in case."

"No one's in the hall and the window is covered by

that heavy curtain. Don't go paranoid on me."

"And don't YOU ever question my authority," she said with a chilling edge to her voice. "You have no idea what I'm capable of, and you NEVER want to find out."

I waited, expecting Mitch to come back with some sarcastic remark, but there was no reply. Grandmotherly Mrs. Corvit had bullied ex-con Mitch into silence.

"Mitch, take the suitcases to the car," Mrs. Corvit ordered. "You can't use the trunk, so put them in the backseat." Then she murmured low, "Now where did I leave my purse?"

"Over there, on the floor," Mitch said, then grunted as he lifted suitcases.

Mrs. Corvit walked across the room, passing inches from me, toward her purse. I tilted my head slightly and stared at the white-leather purse. Blurring vision plagued me again, so I really concentrated as I focused. And this time, without a doubt, I was seeing past the white leather, into the purse. Keys, makeup, a brush, plastic gloves, tissues, museum tickets, two pill bottles, a gun—

A GUN!

Struggling to stay calm, I looked beyond the gun, peering into the folded depths of a slim lavender wallet. A checkbook, credit cards, and green bills inside, twenties and fifties, more than I could count. A California driver's license with a Monterey post office box . . . But wait a minute! Mrs. Corvit had said she was from New York.

And then I saw the name on the driver's license.

Not Eleanor Corvit, but a name I immediately recognized.

A name that shot new terror through me.

Geneva Victor.

NINE

Los Angeles, CA

Serena couldn't stop staring at the coffin. What in the world was a COFFIN doing on the roof? Why would anyone leave such a weird thing in an even weirder place? And then the biggest question.

Was it an EMPTY coffin?

Or was someone inside?

A dead someone.

"Well, it ain't none of my business," Serena told herself, backing away. "Doesn't pay to get involved. Haven't done it before and won't do it now. Gotta look out for me."

And yet she couldn't stop staring at the coffin. The last time she'd seen one had been at her great-aunt Helen's funeral. The casket had been closed, since her aunt had died in a fire. And yet at the funeral, Serena had a sick urge to peek inside the casket, a morbid curiosity that she'd resisted.

That same morbid curiosity prodded and persisted now, nagging at Serena to move forward and take a peek. Just a quick peek. What could it hurt? There couldn't really be anyone inside. That would be TOO weird.

One step closer, another, and then another.

Serena bit her lip, uncertain, yet too curious now to turn back.

Maybe it wasn't a real coffin. Yeah, she thought, it must be a theatrical stage prop that one of the acts left behind. Hadn't there been a magician working here last month? Majestic, or something like that. He had nowhere near the star power of Ravage, but audiences always flocked to see magic.

Majestic had probably put his "lovely assistant" into the coffin, sawed it in half or shish-kebobbed it with "real" swords, then opened the lid, whereupon out popped the assistant, safe and sound, without any missing body parts. A lame act, in Serena's opinion. None of that magic stuff was real.

She took a few more footsteps, stopping at the edge of the coffin, which looked VERY real. An illusion, she assured herself. Reaching out, she lightly ran her fingers over the gleaming, polished wood. Hard, smooth, and cool.

Her fingers drifted down to the bottom edge of the lid and she hesitated, unsure and yet filled with excited curiosity. This wasn't like her aunt's funeral, where mourners were crowded into a small, stuffy room. She was alone up here on the roof. She could peek into the coffin and no one would know. Ever.

So she grasped the lid and pushed upward. It was

heavier than she'd imagined, as if it had been fashioned from expensive, rich wood. Clearly, the coffin was more extravagant than the average prop.

Serena lifted higher, now glimpsing silky gold-satin padding and something pale white—two hands clasped across a still chest. A body. A REAL body, which meant this was a REAL coffin.

And then Serena's gaze drifted higher . . . to the person . . . and she nearly screamed.

NO! It couldn't be . . . Not him!

And yet there was no denying it.

The body belonged to the megastar who would never again shine on stage: the one, the only, the very dead Ravage.

TEN

I was dead meat if Geneva Victor found me!

Varina had described Geneva as a cold, greedy woman who would do anything for money. She was some kind of scientist and carried a briefcase full of needles, tubes, and knives. No way did I want to be experimented on like a biology project.

And I remembered what Eleanor/Geneva had said to Mitch: "Thank goodness we were able to learn what we needed in only three interviews." Which meant they MUST know I was a clone. But how had they guessed? Did they know something I didn't about my past? Or had they somehow glimpsed the "229B" tattoo on my ankle?

Varina and Chase had number tattoos, too. And probably the missing Sandee had one as well. Only Allison lacked the odd tattoo, but the scar on her ankle was proof she'd had some kind of mark at one time.

All of these thoughts ran through my head in mere seconds, while Geneva picked up her purse, retrieved her wig, and left the room.

When the door shut behind her, I let out the biggest, shakiest breath of relief.

I was safe!

Still, I waited a few minutes before I crawled from under the bed. I stood up, put my glasses back on, and stared at the shoe in my hand. In a way it had saved my life, and yet it belonged to HER. With a shudder, I tossed it on the floor.

I went to the door, opened it a crack, and peeked down the hall. No one was in sight. So I crept out, taking soft, slow steps, until I reached the parlor, just in time to see the front door closing behind Geneva and Mitch.

Now what should I do? I wondered. Call the police? But what would I report? I didn't have any proof of wrongdoing, only wild guesses and fears. No crime had been committed. Sure, Geneva Victor had discovered where I was living, but she hadn't tried to hurt me. Yet.

So what was her goal? Why hire "muscle" like Mitch if she only wanted to locate the clones? What did they have planned? I had a feeling a big piece was missing from this puzzle. But at least I was okay and hadn't been caught snooping. I might be a klutz, but today I'd been a lucky klutz.

By now my parents would be back in town with the whole family, getting ready to watch Angel Kristyn in the parade. I couldn't call the police, not without revealing my birth secret, but I could surefire warn my parents.

So I left the bed-and-breakfast, blinking at the darkness that had fallen while I huddled under bedsprings.

It was cold outside, too, and I wished I'd worn a heavy coat.

Hearing the rumble of an engine, I turned and saw a gray car with suitcases piled in the backseat pulling out of the parking lot. Geneva Victor, wearing her grandmotherly gray wig, was at the wheel beside Mitch. Without even glancing in my direction, they drove past, heading away from town. Where were they going? Were they leaving? I hoped so, but I doubted it.

No time to waste. I HAD to tell my parents.

So I took off running, just like earlier today when I'd been trying to save Renegade. Only now I was the one in danger.

I headed for the glow of the millions of lights that illuminated the streets. It was later than I'd realized. The parade would be starting soon.

Turning a corner, I saw a lineup of beautifully lit floats and large groups of band members, horseback riders bejeweled in holiday lights, and swarms of people eager to see the parade. There were too many floats to spot Kristyn's, but when I passed my high school marching band, I saw Larry Joe talking to one of his pals.

"Hey, Larry Joe!" I yelled, having to scream loudly to be heard over the warming-up instruments and cacophony of voices.

He turned in his wheelchair, and waved me over. "Hey, Eric. How come it took so long to deliver a camera? Mom and Dad were looking for you."

"Sorry. But I kind of got stuck." I wiped sweat from my forehead. "Where are Mom and Dad?"

"By the bleachers. They found a good spot to watch the parade."

"Okay. I've got to talk to them NOW."

"What's up?" Larry Joe looked at me quizzically. "Is something wrong? You're acting weirder than normal."

"I don't have time to talk about it, but yeah, something's wrong." I frowned, then turned and dove into the crowd to find my parents.

But just then the parade started moving.

Horses surged forward, elaborate electric floats flashed by, and I was stuck on the wrong side of the street. Just to get across to the bleachers, I'd have to join the parade.

Excited shouts mingled with music and moving vehicles. A cavalry of horses clip-clopped by a few yards in front of me, and I moved forward, jostled by cheerful parade-watchers as I desperately looked for a way to cross the street.

Finally the horses passed, followed by a lively troupe of clowns with bright painted faces, red noses, and flying balloon bouquets. One clown darted toward the crowd, holding out some balloons.

Impulsively, I lunged forward and took the balloons, then "joined" the clowns in the parade. A few of the balloons were the long, twisty type, so while I maneuvered my way across the street, I pasted on a "parade smile" and twisted the balloons into the shape of a hat, which I perched on my head. Not much of a costume, but it did the trick.

When I reached the other side of the street, I took off my balloon hat and placed it on the head of a little girl with black braids.

I saw the bleachers up ahead and hurried toward them, scanning the crowds for my family. Yes, there they were!

"Mom! Dad!" I hollered, making my way through the crowd.

"There you are, Eric." Mom wrapped her arms around me. "We were getting worried."

Dad's arms held on to my youngest sister, who was perched high on his shoulders. "Glad you finally made it."

"But I almost didn't!" I paused to gulp in some air. "They nearly FOUND me!"

"Who?" Mom asked.

"Eleanor and Mitch. Only that's not who they really are, at least not Eleanor; I don't know about Mitch."

"Simmer down, son," Dad said with a disapproving look. "You're not making any sense."

"I know." I took a deep breath, bending over to lean against my knees. "It's confusing. I don't know how to make sense of it myself."

"Start at the begin—," Dad said, only he stopped when Mom suddenly jumped up and squealed excitedly.

"LOOK!" Mom started waving her hands. "There's Kristyn's float!"

Dad lifted my little sister higher on his shoulders and peered at the slow-moving float that had been fashioned on the bed of a one-ton truck, resembling a glittering manger.

"But Mom and Dad—," I said, only they weren't listening.

I'd have to wait till Kristyn's float passed to get their attention, but I supposed a few more minutes wouldn't kill me. So I lifted my head and looked at the float, too. Kristyn might be "The Pain," but she was my sister, and it was cool that she'd been selected to be on a float this year. I figured I might as well cheer her on.

"Where is she? I can't see her," Mom was saying. "Which one of the angels is Kristyn?"

"Can't tell with them dancing around so much," Dad muttered.

With my glasses, I couldn't see Kristyn either. So I took them off, waited a few seconds for the dizziness to pass, then peered into the distance. The "Manger Scene" float featured costumed wise men, barnyard animals, and angels who smiled and waved. The more I stared, the more details I could see. One of the wise men rubbed his chapped and reddened hands to keep warm. And the person at the front end of the cow costume stumbled away from the back-end person when the float hit a sudden bump.

I focused on the angels. Five of them, but only one had long dark hair. Her golden wings sparkled with white lights and her skin glittered with silver body paint.

Only this girl had blue eyes and light skin.

She wasn't my sister.

Where WAS Kristyn?

A frightening thought popped into my head. Eleanor/ Geneva had said she'd learned enough from only three interviews. I'd assumed she'd been talking about me— but maybe not.

The only identifying clone mark was my ankle tattoo: the tattoo that Kristyn had copied on her own ankle. What if Geneva had seen Kristyn's ankle?

And then I remembered something else. When Geneva had ordered Mitch to put the suitcases in the back of the car, she'd said they couldn't use the trunk.

But why couldn't they use the trunk?

Was there already something inside . . . or SOME-ONE?

ELEVEN

It didn't take long for my parents to realize Kristyn wasn't on the float. And when one of my sister's friends said Kristyn hadn't shown up at float practice, my parents were stunned.

"But we dropped her off and watched her walk toward the float," Mom cried with disbelief. "How could she just vanish?"

"Maybe she got nervous about being in front of a crowd," Dad suggested.

"This is Kristyn we're talking about. She LOVES crowds. All she's been talking about for weeks is being an angel on the float. There's no way in the world she would have missed it." Mom's voice cracked and she leaned against Dad for support.

"Don't worry. We'll find her," Dad said, sounding confident despite the panic in his eyes.

Fear knotted in my stomach and I had the mental image of the gray car driving away—the large trunk shut tightly.

Had Kristyn been concealed inside?

"Mom, Dad, there's something you should know."

When I told them that Eleanor Corvit was actually Geneva Victor in disguise, their shock changed to fear. Dad's eyes brimmed with tears and he went to call the police. My mother refused to believe Kristyn was in danger, so she ran through the crowd, looking for her.

I searched with Mom, asking friends and strangers if they'd seen Kristyn. But no one had seen my sister. Around us the festive parade went on, with marching bands blasting holiday songs, clowns waving balloons, and electrifying floats lighting up the night.

"She HAS to be here somewhere," Mom insisted, raking her fingers through her dark blond hair.

"Sure, Mom. We'll keep looking."

"We can't give up, Eric."

"Okay. Let's try by the school where Kristyn was dropped off. Maybe she's there waiting for us."

"Yes . . . yes! Do you really think so?" Mom asked hopefully.

"It's worth a try."

So we headed for the school, the parade sounds dimming behind us. The air was chilly, stinging my hands and ears, but I ignored my discomfort. More than anything, I wanted Kristyn to be at the school.

But deep down I knew my sister had been kidnapped.

Varina, Chase, and Allison had warned me that staying with my family might put them in danger. But I had felt safe with my parents, and had been confident we were safe together.

I'd been wrong.

And now Kristyn was missing.

When we reached the school, there were a few cars parked in the lot, but no one was around. Mom rushed ahead, toward the grassy area where Kristyn had planned to go for float rehearsal.

I hung back, looking around at the decorated buildings, quiet sidewalks, and towering trees. The only movements were shifting shadows and branches that swayed in the breeze. I wondered if there was anything beyond the shadows, so I reached up and took off my glasses.

Blinking till my vision cleared, I peered around again, now seeing a completely different view. My gaze zoomed inside the twinkling decorative holiday lights strung along buildings and into the cracked veins in the sidewalk.

While Mom continued to shout out my sister's name, I stared into dark corners by walls, trees, and shadows. There was nothing unusual at first, but then something glittered.

"Mom!" I called, starting to run toward a dense line of trees. "Over here!"

My head spun dizzily and I nearly stumbled as the sidewalk dipped into damp grass. I put my glasses back on, shutting off my sharp vision, keeping my focus straight ahead. When I reached the trees, I dodged between two arched, bent branches until I found the glittering object.

Then I choked back horror.

No! It couldn't be . . . and yet it was. Among leaves and grass were broken bits of colored glass, gold glitter sprinkled like confetti, and a large, twisted, wire-fashioned wing.

The crushed golden wing was from Kristyn's angel costume.

TWELVE

Hours later, police were combing the school site and Kristyn's picture was being flashed across TV sets. They called it a "possible abduction"—terrifying words. But instead of showing Geneva Victor's picture on the screens, there was an artist's sketch of gray-haired, pudgy, wrinkled "Eleanor Corvit," who was described as a possible witness.

"But that's wrong! There is no Eleanor Corvit!" I insisted to Dad in the hallway after the police left our house. "Why wouldn't you let me tell the police who she really is?"

"Keep it down, Eric." Dad put his finger to his lips, glancing toward the bedrooms. "I don't want your sisters and brothers to hear. I'm only trying to protect you."

"Protect Kristyn. She's the one in danger. The police need to know that Eleanor is really Geneva."

"Eric's right." Mom looked up from the couch, where

she'd been quietly sobbing and wiping her eyes. "We have to tell the whole truth. Or we may . . . may never see Kristyn. . . ." Mom's shoulders shook and she buried her face back into a pillow.

Dad clasped his hands together, his expression grave and heartbreaking. "We can't allow Eric's past to become public knowledge."

"Don't worry about me," I told him.

"I can't help but worry, and for good reason." Dad gave me a deep, harsh look. "Do you have any idea what would happen if people knew you were a clone?"

"It doesn't matter." I reached down to pat Renegade, who sat loyally by my side.

"The media would hound you, snapping pictures and making up wild stories. You couldn't go to school, or even to the grocery store. Folks everywhere would be watching you, wondering, suspicious, and afraid."

"Afraid of what?" I asked.

"You, son." Dad put his arm around my shoulder and held me tight. "Anyone different is a threat to most folks. And being a clone is mighty different. You couldn't live a normal life anymore. People might even believe you had supernatural powers."

"Yeah," I said, touching my glasses, glad I'd kept my vision experiments to myself. "I'm just a regular kid."

"Which is what I want you to be," Dad said firmly. "That's why we can't let anyone know about your birth."

"But what about Kristyn?" Mom demanded. "Lies won't help the police find her."

"Hopefully the police will be able to track down the car from the license plate," Dad pointed out.

"And if they can't?" my mother retorted.

Dad's face crumpled and he sagged into a chair, his

tall frame seeming small and helpless. "I don't have the answers. Having one child missing is . . . terrible. I can't risk Eric, too."

"But what if it's the only way to get Kristyn back!" Mom exclaimed with a fury I'd never seen in my whole life. My parents never EVER argued.

"I'm sorry, honey." Dad put his arms around Mom, but she shook him off.

"Then let Eric tell the police everything!" Mom raged. "Do whatever it takes to find Kristyn."

"I can't." Dad's forehead creased and he shook his head. "I just can't."

"Then I have nothing more to say to you!" Mom swept off the couch and stormed down the hall, the slam of her bedroom door shaking the family portraits on the walls.

Dad sank deeper into the chair and gave an anguished moan, and then his head dropped into his hands. The big, strong man I'd looked up to my entire life was suddenly bruised and broken.

I couldn't bear to watch.

My fault. All my fault.

Since Dad wouldn't let me be honest with the police, I'd have to help Kristyn some other way. I didn't know exactly how, but there was someone who could give me advice.

So I pulled out the scrap of paper with a phone number I still carried in my pocket, went to the phone, and dialed.

THIRTEEN

"Eric?" Allison exclaimed through the phone lines. "Is it really you? I'm SO glad you called. But it's past midnight in your time zone. Isn't this kind of late?"

"It's late, all right," I said grimly. "Hopefully not TOO late."

"Something's wrong?"

"Yeah."

"Are you in trouble?"

"Not me. It's my sister . . . Kristyn." I took a deep breath, then slowly told Allison the whole awful story. It felt good sharing it with someone who really understood.

"Poor Kristyn!" Allison cried softly. "How horrible!"

"It wouldn't have happened if it weren't for me."

"It's not your fault, Eric."

"Kristyn is gone because she copied my tattoo."

"Just a tattoo isn't enought proof," Allison pointed

out. "There has to be more. What does Kristyn look like?"

"Pretty, I guess. She's fifteen like me and almost as tall as you. She's part Asian, with long black hair and dark eyes."

"Oh, no!" Allison exclaimed. "That explains it."

"What?"

"I saw a picture of Sandee Yoon and she has long black hair, black eyes, and golden skin. They kidnapped Kristyn because they think she's Sandee."

"The missing clone?" I asked, surprised I hadn't guessed this myself.

"It makes sense. Geneva and her accomplice found out one of the clones was in Texas. Maybe they traced the credit card or the airline tickets from when we visited. They knew about Chase, Varina, and me, but after Dr. Victor's arrest it was too risky to pursue us. So they went after you and Sandee."

"And when they saw the tattoo on Kristyn's ankle, they jumped to the wrong conclusion," I guessed, feeling more guilty than ever. "Kristyn wouldn't even have that tattoo if she wasn't trying to be like me. She really admires me. But instead of being nice to her, I only called her names."

"Brothers insults sisters. That's normal."

"But I'm NOT normal," I cried. "And you, Varina, Chase, and Sandee aren't either. That's what caused this trouble. Kristyn would be home asleep in her bed right now if I weren't her brother."

"Cut out the self-pity, and let's figure how to find your sister."

"I can't tell the police about Geneva Victor without revealing I'm a clone."

"So any ideas what you can do?"

"Find Kristyn myself," I said firmly, the idea coming to me suddenly. And I knew it was the best solution. "I got Kristyn into this mess, so it's up to me to find her."

"Having incredible eyesight doesn't make you a superhero, any more than my strength makes me one."

"I know. But I have to find Kristyn before something bad happens."

"Then let me help. Varina and Chase, too. We can be like clone crusaders," she added with a wry laugh.

"Crusading is kind of hard when you're in California and I'm in Texas."

"That's for sure. Besides, no one knows where Geneva and that Mitch guy are. They could be in another country by now."

"I don't think so," I said.

"Why not?"

"Geneva has a California driver's license, and I also learned something interesting while hiding in her room."

"When you saw into her purse?" Allison asked.

"Before that," I replied. "I was holding a clue in my hand, only I didn't know it then. And it could be JUST the clue to lead me to Kristyn."

FOURTEEN

Instead of sleeping that night, I embarked on a cyber-search.

My brothers were sound sleepers, so they didn't even stir when I booted up my computer. Some of the information I needed would take special "hacking" talents. I wasn't one of those hacker types who could crack passwords and sneak into secret files, but I had a few friends who were. One of them, a cyberpal who went by the nickname of Sam (I didn't know his real name or where he lived), owed me a favor for helping him reach Level 12 of the Moon Invaders RPG game. So my first plan of action was to send an SOS E-mail to Sam asking him for information on the Victors and Mitch Crouch.

It could take minutes or hours to hear from Sam, so I switched to a search engine and keyed in the words "Pacific Soles."

Eleanor Corvit may have claimed to come from New

York, but Geneva Victor had bought the silver shoes at a store near the Pacific Ocean and her license listed a Monterey post office address. If the Victors were as rich as Varina claimed, they probably owned several houses and properties. I was betting that one of their homes was in Monterey. The more I could learn, the closer I'd be to finding my sister.

My sister. The horror of the situation hit me, and I prayed she was okay. I was fairly sure Geneva wouldn't harm Kristyn. Not yet, anyway. Geneva would take Kristyn somewhere private to do experiments. Scalpels, needles, and frightening drugs. I shuddered. Kristyn had spent most of her life dealing with hospitals and chemotherapy. She'd survived leukemia. But would she survive THIS?

The computer whirled and showed three matches for Pacific Soles. One was a newspaper article from a Monterey paper advertising, "Step into yesterday's elegant styles with today's hottest shoe boutique." The other two entries both led to the website for "Pacific Soles, Shoes for the Soul."

A few clicks of my keyboard and I'd checked out the website, not bothering to download images of shoes, instead focusing on the address, which described the location as just a short drive from downtown Monterey.

"YES! I knew it!" I whispered, pumping my arm in the air. Then I jotted down the address and phone number on a Post-it note. Someone at the store was sure to know Geneva. Maybe she had a whole other identity I had yet to discover.

Then I went back to the *Real Families* website I'd bookmarked, and jotted down its address and number, too. It was a long shot, probably a totally bogus connection, but I had to be thorough.

Next I went to a People Search and tried a variety of name combinations: Geneva Victor, Dr. Mansfield Victor, Eleanor Corvit, Mitch Crouch, Geneva Corvit, Mitchell Crouch, or wilder combinations like Geneva Mansfield, Eleanor Crouch, or Dr. Victor Mansfield. I tried everything I could think of, then spent the next few hours sorting through garbage listings, gaining only a few solid facts.

By the time the sun crept through my window, causing me to blink and yawn, my head was swimming with bits and pieces like fragments from mismatched puzzles.

I knew Geneva Victor had shopped "just a short drive" from Monterey, California. I'd found a few newspaper clippings about Dr. Victor's "gun incident" involving "an unnamed teenage girl" and also some articles about charity functions the Victors attended in Los Angeles, St. Louis, and Chicago. The Chicago charity function was dated two weeks AFTER the "gun incident" with Varina. So obviously Dr. Victor was NOT in prison. But that didn't tell me where he was now and why his wife was posing as an old woman.

My head throbbed and my eyes ached. I leaned back in my chair and closed my eyes, just to rest for a minute.

I must have fallen asleep. I had no sense of time passing, but suddenly I felt a tug behind me, and then I was falling backward in the chair. . . .

THUMP and CRASH! I landed on the floor with my feet poking up in the air. And from behind me I heard familiar chuckles. My brothers were awake and acting like total jerks as usual.

"You were drooling in your sleep, Eric," Marcos teased.

"Only computer geeks sleep at their computers,"

Larry Joe said with a snort, rolling his wheelchair toward the large closet.

I righted myself and scowled at my brothers. "I was looking for information to help Kristyn."

Immediately, my brothers stopped smiling.

"Kristyn's still missing?" Marcos asked.

"But I thought she'd be back by now," Larry Joe said, his strong shoulders slumping in his chair.

I shook my head sadly.

Turning away from them, I reached for my computer mouse and checked my E-mail. Five messages had come in while I slept: three from my role-playing list-serve, one piece of junk mail advertising a way to make a million dollars, and one from Sam.

I clicked on Sam's message and read:

> "YO, RIC—WACKED REQUEST, BUT I'M ON IT.
> MY CYBERCLAWS ARE SHARPENED AND I'M HACK-
> ING AWAY. GOTTA SAY I'M CURIOUS. BUT HEY,
> IT'S YOUR BIZ. SAM."

No results yet, but I could count on Sam. He'd find out financial, professional, and legal information about the Victors and Mitch Crouch. I just had to wait.

Unfortunately, waiting was the name of the game at our house.

I found my father in the dining room, pouring cereal for the two youngest kids, but no sign of Mom. Oh, no. Either Mom was too upset to leave her room or she and Dad still weren't speaking.

We usually went to church as a family on Sunday, but Dad said we'd skip today. We had to stick by the phone in case there was any news about Kristyn.

So when the phone rang, everyone jumped . . . and then froze in place. It was Dad who strode into the kitchen and snatched the receiver before it rang a third time.

"Yes?" he said roughly. There was a long, tense pause as he listened. Then he asked, "You've found the car?"

I knew without a doubt they were talking about the gray rental car. I scooted close to Dad so I could hear better.

"What about my daughter? . . . I see . . . But can't you—? Oh, you did already . . . What about finger-prints?" Dad clutched the phone so tightly, his knuckles were bone-white. "Okay, I understand. But you have to do more than that . . . Well . . ." Dad wiped sweat from his brow and seemed to be thinking hard. "Well, there's a woman you should check out."

Startled, I held my breath.

Dad continued, "Her name is Geneva Victor."

I gasped. What was Dad doing? Was he going to reveal my past?

"No, Detective Peters." Dad shook his head. "I don't know this woman, but she might have seen something. . . . Yeah, a possible witness . . . Will you? That would be great. Thanks."

Then Dad hung up and let out a shaky breath. "I decided it wouldn't hurt to mention the Victor woman," he admitted.

"I'm glad you did," I told him.

"Your secret will be safe," Dad assured me. "No one has to find out WHY that woman was in town."

"I'm not worried." I tried to sound confident. "So they found the gray car?"

"Yup. Deserted outside of town. There are tracks of another car, but otherwise it's a dead end."

"Geneva switched cars," I muttered angrily. "It'll be harder to follow her trail."

"The police think she's headed for New York, because of that TV show she claimed to work for."

"But they're wrong!"

"We have to trust the police." Dad's voice cracked. "They're doing their best to find her. They're our only hope. . . ."

"No they aren't." I shook my head firmly. "They don't even know why Kristyn was taken, but I do. I'm the one who can find Kristyn."

"How?" He sounded skeptical.

"I was talking to Allison and—"

"Allison?" Dad blinked, confused. "Who? Oh . . . that blond girl . . . one of THEM."

If I hadn't been so exhausted and worried, I might have pointed out to Dad that I was "one of THEM," too. Instead I blurted out the plan. "I think Kristyn is being taken to California. Maybe Monterey. And I want to go there to look for her."

"California?" Dad nearly knocked over a box of cereal. "You can't be serious!"

"I am. Very."

"And how do you propose getting there?" he asked with heavy sarcasm. "It's a mighty long walk and you're too young to drive."

"Fly." I clenched my hands together. "Allison offered to make my airline reservation."

"You will NOT allow that girl to pay your way. It's out of the question."

"I have to go." I folded my arms and pursed my lips. "And you can't change my mind."

"I sure as hell can!" Dad's blue eyes blazed, as if all his fear had blended into solid anger, directed at me.

"You're not going anywhere, except your room. You can just stay there till I say so. And no more making long-distance calls without my permission!"

"But you don't understand—"

"I understand you're defying your father, and I won't stand for it. Now get to your room."

My shoulders slumped.

I turned, and went to my room.

FIFTEEN

I had failed before I'd even had a chance to try. And worse—I couldn't even call Allison, not without Dad's permission.

So I returned to my computer.

No new E-mail from Sam. Totally discouraged, I aimlessly killed time by zapping aliens with deadly lasers. I reached Level 23 and saved the Empire of Yurvania, the highest level I'd ever reached. But I felt no thrill.

When I checked my E-mail again, I was rewarded with a message from Sam.

"YES!" I cried, then opened the message.

"YO, RIC—NOTHING ON MITCH CROUCH, BUT THAT VICTOR DUDE IS REALLY ROLLING IN IT. $$$ AND LOTS OF DULL ARTICLES IN SNOOTY DOCTOR JOURNALS. ALSO SOME KIND OF SCANDAL WITH A TEENAGE GIRL, BUT HE BOUGHT A 'GET OUT OF

JAIL' CARD. I GOT THE LIST OF PROPERTY YOU
WANTED, ONLY NOTHING IN MONTEREY. ALSO,
LOTS OF LA-DE-DAH CHARITY EVENTS G.V. AT-
TENDED. SEE ATTACHMENTS. SAM."

I clicked on the attachments and found newspaper
clippings of charity events, one showing the smiling
faces of Geneva and Dr. Victor. I immediately recognized Geneva, with her short stylish dark hair, pleasant
smile, and determined lift of her chin. But Dr. Victor
was a surprise. He was much older than Geneva, looking
more like her father than her husband. He was Hispanic,
bald, and wore glasses, a gentle, harmless-looking man.
Of course, I knew different. . . .

I opened up the next attachment. A list of property
the Victors owned. Three were located in California, but
like Sam said, nothing in Monterey. Darn. Still, I studied
the three listings:

> #1. Fifty-five acres, investment property, Red
>   Bluff
> #2. Three-bedroom apartment, San Jose
> #3. Condo, rental property, Pacific Grove

I stared at the third entry, feeling a glimmer of excitement. And a quick map check proved my hunch
right. The condo in Pacific Grove was only "a short
drive to downtown Monterey." Just like the ad for Pacific Soles advertised.

I was getting close. Kristyn was either on her way to
California or already there, I could feel it. It was amazing how much information you could find in cyberspace.
Being confined to my room wasn't nearly the punish-
ment Dad had intended.

The next two attachments were copies of articles from science journals written by Dr. Mansfield Victor: "Ethics For Artificial Growth of Human Organs" and "Designer Genes: Profit or Progress?" Both topics gave me chills, proving a clear interest in genetic cloning.

Reading through the articles only added to my unease. Dr. Victor's views were very clinical, citing scientific reasons for continued research, but downplaying the human factor. He stressed careful selection of compatible donor genes and explained the medical benefits of harvesting artificial livers, limbs, and skin. In conclusion, he boasted of the advancements he was making in his own research, and hinted at amazing discoveries he expected to announce soon.

I hoped I wasn't one of his "amazing discoveries." No way was that sicko doctor going to experiment on me. And I wouldn't let him or his wife harm Kristyn either. But first I had to find Kristyn. . . .

From outside my room, I heard the phone ring.

My hands, poised over the keyboard, stopped in midair, and without hesitation I jumped up and raced out of my room. Who was on the phone? Was it news of Kristyn? Or maybe Allison was calling back.

When I entered the kitchen, I knew instantly by the tense edges of Dad's shoulders and his heavy tone that he was talking to Detective Peters again. And that it wasn't good news.

". . . but that can't be true," Dad said gravely. "I was told she'd been here in town . . . Are you sure?" Dad's brow furrowed. "Well, I guess I was mistaken. Yeah . . . Please do let us know when you hear some news. Thanks for everything."

Hanging up, Dad wiped his eyes, then slowly turned

and noticed me. His frown deepened. "What are you doing out of your room?"

"I heard the phone." I bit my lip and asked quietly, "What's happening? Couldn't they find Geneva Victor?"

"Oh, they found her, all right," he said angrily. "She and her husband have been vacationing in Mexico for a week."

"No!" I cried. "But I saw her. She was HERE!"

"You were wrong." Dad glared at me. "And I've had enough of your wild stories."

"I was telling the truth."

"Your truth doesn't fit with the facts, so leave the investigating to the police." Dad ran his fingers through his dark, mussed hair and softened his tone. "Eric, I don't mean to take my frustration out on you. It's just that I feel so helpless."

"Then let me help."

"The best way for you to help is to stay out of it. The police are checking some leads and the FBI is involved now, too. The professionals will find Kristyn. All we can do is wait."

"But Dad—"

"Enough, Eric!" He raised his hand, silencing me. "Please, go back to your room."

I started to argue, only what was the use? Dad wouldn't believe me, even though I knew without a doubt he was wrong. The best way to help wasn't for me to stay out of it, but for me to take action—drastic action.

I was going after Kristyn.

Tonight.

SIXTEEN

My backpack was stuffed with clothes and other ne-
cessities. I wore dark jeans, a black shirt, and a navy-
blue denim jacket.

I left, sneaking out of the bedroom I shared with Marcos and Larry Joe, tiptoeing down the hall and through
the living room, then slipping out the back door. The
night sky was cooperating, offering a scattering of
clouds to soften the bright stars and half-moon, enough
light to see by and yet plenty of shadows to hide in.

The hardest part of my plan would be getting to the
bus station. It was a long drive into town, and an even
longer walk. Since I couldn't drive yet and didn't want
to walk, I'd decided to use my bike.

As I stepped into the chilly night, I congratulated myself on having managed to sneak out unseen. Then I
heard a rustling of bushes and a loud, playful bark. Oh,

no! I thought as Renegade bounded over to my side. Just the kind of help I didn't need!

"Go away, Renegade," I said softly.

Hearing his name, the dog wagged his tail and licked my hand.

"No, boy." I tried to sound firm. "Back to your doghouse. Go on, Renegade."

He barked and jumped in the air, clearly deciding this was a fun new game.

"Quiet, Ren. You'll give me away!"

His answer was a big doggy slurp on my hand and more tail-wagging. Geez, now what was I going to do? I couldn't let him follow me.

With a heavy sigh, I firmly grabbed Renegade's collar. If I put him inside the house, he'd wake up my parents, so my only recourse was to lock him in the garage.

"Sorry, boy," I said as I opened the garage door and pushed him inside. "I can't risk you following me."

Renegade wiggled his tail and slurped my hand again.

"I mean it. You're staying here."

He tried to dodge around my legs, but I blocked his way.

"Someone will let you out in the morning. Now be a good boy and go to sleep." Then I shut the door.

As I turned to leave, I heard Renegade's pitiful whine, but I steeled my heart. He would be fine. I couldn't be so sure about my sister. I crossed my fingers and whispered, "I'm coming, Kristyn. Be safe till I get there."

Kristyn HAD to be in California. The driver's license and condo in Pacific Grove were proof. The police could be fooled by the Victors, but not me. I was determined to find my sister . . . no matter what.

So I walked away from the garage toward the small

shed where Mom kept gardening tools, Dad kept the lawn mower, and I kept my bike.

I grasped the handlebars and tapped the kickstand with my foot. As I started to climb onto my bike, I heard a twig crunch behind me.

Before I could turn to look, rough fingers grabbed my arm and jerked me backward. My feet slipped, and my bike and I crashed to the ground. . . .

SEVENTEEN

Los Angeles, CA

Serena nearly fell over in shock.

Ravage dead! It couldn't be true! And yet he wasn't breathing or moving, and he WAS inside a coffin. There was no other explanation. Death wasn't a magician's trick—it was the real thing!

Tears fell down Serena's cheeks, and she remembered her foster mother admitting that she cried when Elvis died. At the time, Serena thought it was lame to cry over a singer. But now she understood. Ravage was more than a singer: he was an icon loved by millions. And now he would never sing again.

Serena stared at the pale, still body. This was way too creepy. But she needed to think clearly. A coffin, corpse, and deserted rooftop were a BAD combo. She had to get out of here—FAST.

Slamming the coffin lid, Serena turned and hurried through the narrow wall passage. But she had to stop when she reached the same locked door. Maybe it was only stuck, not locked. She reached out to try again, only before she could touch it, the knob MOVED.

Her first thought was, Hey! I'm rescued! But then a chilling possibility stabbed her mind. What if the person turning the knob was the same person who'd killed Ravage and then put him in a coffin? A murderer!

I am SO out of here! Serena determined. Then before the door could open, she ran, not having any clue where she was headed.

The roof truly was a maze, with confusing twists and sharp turns. Her footsteps echoed in her ears as she ran. Only now she also heard another set of pounding footsteps: heavier, faster, and headed her way.

The killer had returned!

And now he was chasing HER!

Panic spurred Serena to move even faster. She saw a large outcropping up ahead with a narrow opening, and she dived for it, then ducked through a slim tunnel and scrambled forward.

Behind her she heard a thud and a groan, as if her pursuer had bumped into something. Good! She hoped he had hurt himself badly.

But then his footsteps pounded again. With her breath coming in quick, exhausted gasps, she knew she had to escape, but she felt as if she was running in circles. Where was the door she'd entered through? She had to find it SOON—before the killer found HER.

Aside from her rapid breath and the footsteps, she realized she was hearing another sound: a familiar mechanical hum that seemed to vibrate the concrete beneath her feet. The air-conditioning unit! That's where the humming was coming from, and she remembered seeing the gigantic unit near the entrance door. All she had to do was follow the noise.

More turns, narrow passages, and other obstructions. Then suddenly the air conditioner loomed up ahead, its noise filling her head and drowning out other sounds. She ducked around the unit, then stopped suddenly when she ran into a solid wall.

"No! I can't be trapped!" she cried.

Serena wanted to just curl up and cry, but she refused to surrender. She couldn't hear the pursuing footsteps anymore, but she knew HE was out there, looking for her. And when he found her? What then? Would she be the next dead body in a coffin?

"I will not be a victim," she swore aloud to herself, new fury racing through her. She'd given up being a victim when she'd left Colorado last year. No more boozing foster mother who ranted and raged without warning. And no more living in a nothing town with no chance for stardom. She'd made a new life for herself, cut and colored her hair in a style that added five years to her age, created a new identity. Good-bye, loser Sandee Yoon. Hello, survivor Serena.

So instead of curling up with her tears, Serena searched for a way past the wall. She couldn't go back or around, so she'd go UP. She reached high and stood on her tiptoes, then grasped the top of the wall. Grabbing tight, she pulled herself up, then over, and suddenly there was escape: THE DOOR.

Without any hesitation, she lunged forward and clutched the knob, twisted it easily, and burst through the doorway.

YES!

A stairwell had never looked so wonderful! She took

the stairs two at a time, running down, zooming by the Penthouse, passing the 17th floor, and not stopping until she reached her own floor.

When she swept into the room she shared with Amishka, she was dizzy with relief. "I made it!" she cried, slamming the door behind her and sinking onto the bed.

Amishka, who'd been sitting in a chair with the red-beaded dress spread across her lap, gave Serena a harsh look. "Where have *you* been?"

Serena hesitated, afraid to admit the truth. "You wouldn't believe me if I told you."

"I'm not lame enough to believe half the lies you tell," Amishka said with a scowl. "You left me hanging, running out without fixing this dress, and I gotta go on in a few hours. If you think I'm so unfair to you, then you can just get out."

Serena gave Amishka a startled look. "Oh, Mish! I'm sorry I blew up. I mean, you're the greatest."

"I am?"

"For sure! You've been watching out for me and I appreciate it. Here, let me fix that dress."

"Well . . ." The anger faded from Amishka's purple-shadowed eyes. "You're right. You wouldn't have lasted two minutes if I hadn't taken you in. I've always stood up for you."

"YES! I owe you so much." Serena took the dress and reached for her sewing case, relieved to be alive. "And I know you'll help me sing onstage when you're ready."

"Darned straight, girlfriend," Amishka said, smiling now. "I don't deny you got a good voice. Almost as good as mine. And some night I'm gonna tell Slam to give you a shot."

Suddenly there was a sharp knock on the door.

"Get it, Serena," Amishka ordered.

But Serena froze in place, her threaded needle mid-stitch over the dress. Panic gripped her. What if it was the killer?

More knocks—louder, insistent, impatient.

"Why are you just sitting there, Serena?" Amishka complained. "Fine! I'll do it myself."

"No . . . don't . . . ," Serena whispered, trembling.

But it was too late.

Amishka grabbed the knob and yanked open the door.

Serena took one look at the blond guy standing in the doorway, screamed out "NOOOOOO!" and then promptly collapsed to the floor in a dead faint.

EIGHTEEN

"Eric! Where are you going?" the attacker demanded, and I immediately recognized his voice.

"Larry Joe!" I picked myself and my bike off the ground. I was surprised I hadn't heard my brother's wheelchair coming up behind me on the paved walkway. "You jerk! Why'd you sneak up on me?"

"You're the one sneaking around."

"So what? That's my business."

"I'm making it MY business," he snapped. "I knew you were up to something when I saw you creeping out of our room. What's going on?"

"Nothing."

"You've been acting really strange. And I heard you and Dad arguing earlier."

"Dad's totally unfair. That's why I have to leave." I adjusted the backpack on my shoulders and grabbed the bike's handlebars. "I'm the only one who can find Kristyn."

"You know where she is?" Larry Joe sounded surprised.

"Not exactly, but I know about the people who took her."

"The ones who visited you last month?"

"No way! Allison, Varina, and Chase are my friends. If I need help finding Kristyn, they'll be there for me."

"So how do you know who grabbed Kristyn?" Larry Joe asked, his gaze puzzled as he looked up at me.

"I can't tell." Pursing my lips firmly, I shook my head. "And if you want to help Kristyn, don't ask any more questions. Time's running out. I need to leave."

"On your bike?" he asked skeptically. "Your legs may work better than mine, but you suck at athletics. You won't get very far on a bike. Where do you plan to go?"

I glanced away, not about to share my plans.

"Eric, you can trust me. You're not the only one who cares about Kristyn."

Still, I wouldn't answer. I just wanted Larry Joe to go away. He could ruin everything!

"I'm leaving now," I said stonily, walking the bike toward the driveway. "And don't even think about telling Mom and Dad."

"Eric, you're such a jerk. Why won't you let me help." He rolled his wheelchair quickly, keeping up with me.

"I don't need any help."

"Yes you do, fleabrain. You need something faster than a bike. And I bet you didn't even think about money. Do you have any?"

"Of course."

"How much?" he persisted, making me wish I had the nerve and the muscles to punch the smug expression off his face.

"I have enough money." I thought of the ninety-four dollars and fifty-five cents in my pocket and sighed. "Enough for bus fare . . . I hope."

"Eric, you need my help. Admit it."

"Not a chance. I can do this myself."

"No you can't." Larry Joe wheeled swiftly, coming in front of my bike and forcing me to stop. "And I'm going to help you, whether you want it or not. So just stop arguing and listen to me. Here's what I'm going to do. . . ."

Larry Joe might have been a jerk, but he was a jerk with a driver's license and the ability to operate our custom-made van, which had been designed for physically challenged drivers. He eased the van out of the driveway with the lights off, then switched the lights back on when we reached the main road.

And when he let me off at the bus station, he did something that totally shocked me.

"Here, Eric," he said, pulling out his wallet and handing me a wad of green bills. One hundred and twenty dollars!

I opened my mouth, but no words came out. It was easy to share insults with my brother, but thanks and compliments tasted strange. And I sensed that Larry Joe felt the same way, so we both just nodded.

"I'll pay you back," I promised.

"Find Kristyn. That's all the payback I need. Good luck," Larry Joe said, punching my shoulder.

"You got it." I punched his shoulder back, then waved

as he made a U-turn with the van and drove away. Watching him go, I whispered, "Thank you."

Then I went into the bus station to buy a ticket to California.

NINETEEN

Morning found me squeezed against a bus window and plugging my nose when my seatmate opened a bottle of purple nail polish and began applying it to her VERY long, should-be-registered-as-lethal-weapons fingernails.

I held my breath and tried not to choke on the fumes. Behind me I heard someone say, "What's that SMELL?" But Miss Fingernails kept polishing. I was SO relieved when she grabbed her bags at the next stop, waved a purple-nailed good-bye, and left the bus.

While others headed for rest rooms or grabbed a bite to eat, I took the chance to find a pay phone and make two phone calls.

The first was to my parents. By now they knew I was gone, not only missing school but defying Dad's orders. I took a deep breath and steeled myself for their anger.

Sure enough, Dad's voice erupted through the phone lines with volcanic force. He ordered me to turn around and come home right now, but I refused. I told him I was safe and promised to check in regularly.

Feeling worse than ever, but still determined to see this through, I begged Dad not to come after me. Before he could say yes, no, or get your hide back home, I hung up.

Then I dialed Allison's number. Only I got her danged answering machine again. Geez, if I ever got into politics I'd pass a law against answering machines. I didn't bother leaving a message.

And the bus rolled on . . . and on . . . and on.

I slept most of the time, fatigue and anxiety hitting me hard. In my dreams, I saw Kristyn strapped to a hospital gurney, her mouth covered with tape and a sharp scalpel poised over her. Then the door suddenly burst open, and I rushed in to the rescue. I knocked the scalpel away, tackled the bad guys, released Kristyn, then brought her back home to my family. Kristyn was safe and everyone called me a hero.

But in the bad version of my dream, the door was locked and no matter how hard I tried to break in, I couldn't. Over and over again, I heard Kristyn scream, "Help me, Eric!" When I awoke I was drenched in sweat and my heart was thundering. I was glad when the bus engine slowed, the brakes screeched, and we pulled into another station.

Once again I went to a pay phone, but still Allison didn't answer. I knew I could count on her, but I worried that something was wrong.

The bus didn't leave for thirty minutes, so I went to find some food. My stomach was raw with hunger and worry. Only when I counted out my money, I was dismayed at how little was left after the bus ticket. Though I craved a combo sandwich meal complete with salad, jumbo fries, and a drink, I opted for a thin slice of pep-peroni pizza and a cup of water.

Then back to the bus. This time I lucked out and no one sat beside me. Yawning, I stretched out, using my backpack as a pillow and my jacket as a blanket, and fell into a dreamless sleep.

It was dark when I awoke to screeching brakes and the noisy bustle from the other passengers as they stood and gathered their belongings. I wasn't even sure what state I was in.

Once again, I dragged myself off the bus and found a pay phone. When I dialed Allison's number, it was a shock when she actually picked up.

"ERIC!" she exclaimed. "At last! Your father called and he's a total wreck. He's furious you ran away."

"I didn't run. Although I'm starting to think that run-ning might have been faster than taking the bus."

"Not funny, Eric. Where are you?"

"I'm not sure. Out of Texas, anyway." I glanced at the phone and noticed the address. "Nevada."

"Still hours away," she complained. "You should have let me buy you an airline ticket."

"Wasn't necessary," I said, recognizing Dad's family pride in my tone. "Thanks, Allison, but I'm fine. Just be there waiting when I arrive in San Francisco."

"You got it, even if it means ditching my classes."

"Will you get in trouble?"

"Absolutely!" She laughed. "But no more than usual. And my roommate Lucia will cover for me. I'm not exactly a model student, if you haven't guessed. But it works for me."

I chuckled, wishing I had her confidence. She didn't stumble through life, afraid of falling or making a mistake. Allison's DNA gave her unusual strength, both inside and out.

"By the way, Eric," Allison was saying, her voice becoming serious. "There's something you should know. I heard it on the news a while ago."

"What?" I asked. "About Kristyn?"

"Not her. The FBI investigated Michael Roach."

"Who?" The name meant nothing to me.

"The man who helped kidnap your sister. He used an alias of Mitch Crouch, but Michael Roach is his real name."

"Oh, Mitch. My first impression was right about him. That scum nearly ran over my dog. He only pretended to be sorry. And I overheard Geneva say he'd been in prison."

"The news report called him a wanted felon. They said he had broken his parole and was on the run for a new crime—"

"Something besides kidnapping Kristyn?"

"Yeah." Allison hesitated. "Murder."

"Mitch killed someone!" I gripped the phone so hard that if I'd had Allison's strength it would have snapped in two.

"Yeah. It happened a few weeks ago. He was seen running from an ex-girlfriend's apartment, and inside the apartment, they found her body. . . ." Allison paused. "Her neck was broken. Sorry, but I had to tell you."

I didn't know what to say. I'd known Geneva was bad news, but I had no idea Mitch was even worse. And they had my sister.

Murmuring that I had to go, I hung up the phone. I couldn't get Allison's words out of my head, and the worry I'd had for my sister switched to terror.

I knew without a doubt that if I didn't find Kristyn soon, I'd never see her alive again.

TWENTY

Los Angeles, CA

"A ghost . . . ," Serena moaned, feeling a cold cloth on her face and blinking awake. "He's dead. . . ."

But when Serena opened her eyes, she stared into the VERY alive face of Ravage. Spiked blond hair, hypnotic green eyes, and full lips that girls everywhere dreamed of kissing.

"You okay?" he asked.

"I'm fine, but you're dead." Serena shook her head. "It's YOU. Only it can't be you."

"Most fans just ask for my autograph." He laughed. "No need to faint."

Amishka giggled. "I'll take your autograph."

Serena continued to stare. Ravage wasn't only alive, but he was HERE, in her room, and Amishka was flirting with him. This was just too much.

"I'm sorry for my assistant's behavior," Amishka cooed as she handed Ravage a CD to sign. "Serena can be really dense sometimes, you know? And you spell my name A-M-I-S-H-K-A."

"Lovely name for a luscious babe. How about after my gig tonight we meet somewhere?"

"Oooh!" Amishka squealed, which clearly was a yes. "Name the place, and I'm there yesterday!"

Serena sat up on the couch, her head spinning. "But I saw you DEAD," she murmured. "You were in a coffin."

Ravage draped an arm around Amishka and rolled his eyes. "Your friend must be tripping out. You should take care of her."

"Oh, I will," Amishka said with a dazed, love-struck expression. "Later. Now I'd rather talk to you."

"Same here. But business first, sweet thang. That's what I came here for."

"You did?" Amishka fluffed her silver wig. "What's up?"

"I was looking for your pal Slam, and someone said he might be with you."

"Slam?" Serena rubbed her head. "I was looking for him, too. . . . That's when I found . . ." She stopped, so confused she couldn't think straight. How could Ravage be both dead and alive? Was this some kind of sick joke?

She stared at his face, noticing a jagged scar below one ear. Too, his nose seemed wider and his chin a bit sharper than she remembered.

"Anyway," Ravage told Amishka, "if you see Slam, say I was looking for him."

"I'll find him for you," Amishka offered eagerly.

"No need." He waved his hands. "You must be aw-fully busy."

"Not too busy for YOU, Ravage."

"He's not Ravage," Serena stated, this fact suddenly clear to her. "Oh, he looks like Ravage, but he's an impostor. Can't you tell, Amishka?"

"Serena!" Amishka shrieked. "Of course he's Ravage. Everyone knows that."

"Yeah. Listen to your friend." Ravage (or whoever he was) reached out and grabbed Serena's hand firmly and gave her a dark look. "You have no idea what you're saying."

"Oh, yes I do. I was on the roof and—"

He yanked her toward him. "I can use some help find-ing Slam, after all. And you can take me to him, sweet thang. Amishka, I hope you don't mind if I borrow your assistant."

"Not really, but I'd rather go with you."

"You and I have a date for later tonight," he promised. "I'll see you then."

"Let me go!" Serena tugged and tried to pull away. "I am NOT going with you. Amishka, don't let him take me away."

"Serena, would you grow up?" Amishka snapped, clearly annoyed that Ravage was paying attention to Se-rena. "If Ravage wants your help, then you're gonna help him."

"But—," Serena tried to argue, only Ravage squeezed her wrist so hard tears came to her eyes. He yanked open the door and dragged her into the hallway.

"Let me go!" she sobbed. "Amishka! Help!"

But the door had already shut, leaving Serena alone in the hall with an imposter.

"Shut up," he snarled, dragging her toward the elevator.

"Who are you?"

"Ravage."

"No you aren't. But that's your problem, not mine, and I don't care. Just let me go and I won't tell anyone."

"Can't chance that."

"I'll scream if you don't let me go."

"Go ahead. Girls scream at rock stars all the time. I'll say you're just another whacked-out groupie."

"You creep!" she exclaimed as she twisted and squirmed to break free. Her arms were pinned to her side, so she kicked him in the leg.

"Ouch! Cut that out!"

"I will if you let me go."

"So you can go around telling everyone I'm DEAD?" he demanded angrily. "What if someone believed you? Now shut up or I'll shut you up personally."

Serena answered by giving him an even harder kick, one that caused him to groan and double over in pain.

She ran from the elevator and toward the stairwell. Yanking open the door, she hurried inside and began running up to the 17th floor, hoping to get help from Slam or the other band members. Hearing the metallic echo of her footsteps was like a bitter replay of her run on the roof. Only this time she knew who her pursuer was, or at least who he pretended to be.

But oddly, she didn't hear any footsteps behind her. She stopped and leaned against a rail, looking down the flights of stairs. No one.

Where had Ravage gone? Had he given up following her? Could she be that lucky?

Breathing a sigh of relief, she continued up the stairs, not running anymore, but hurrying nonetheless. Her legs ached and her throat felt raw from gasping for breath. Fortunately she'd always had incredible stamina, so she kept going, not stopping until she reached the 17th floor.

Opening the door marked "17," she burst forward with new energy—and SMACK!

She collided with another person: a tall stranger a few years older than her with white-blond hair and unusual blue-gray eyes. She'd never seen him before in her life, and yet she couldn't take her gaze from his.

"I'm sorry," the blond guy started to say. "Did I hurt you?"

"No." She glanced behind, afraid Ravage would find her. "But I have to go . . . I'm in a hurry—"

"Are you in trouble?" he asked with concern.

"Nothing I can't handle."

"Okay. Then maybe you can help me. I'm looking for Fever Pitch. I was told they were on this floor."

"Yeah. I'm headed there."

"You know Fever Pitch?"

She gave a quick nod, glancing behind nervously, continuing on down the hallway with the blond guy.

"That's great." His smile softened his rugged features. "I'm trying to find a girl who might be staying with them."

"Whatever. Just walk faster. The room's at the end of the hall." Serena glanced behind again, but no one was following.

"This girl I'm looking for, she's from Colorado, fifteen years old, and has long black hair. Maybe you know her."

"WHAT?" Serena stopped, startled by the description, and stared at him. "What's her name?"

"Sandee Yoon."

TWENTY-ONE

"I'll have to sneak you into my room, Eric," Allison told me as she punched the coded sequence on the gate and we entered the impressive grounds of her private school. "Guys aren't allowed above the first floor. And my suite is on the third floor."

"Suite?"

"Oh, that's what they call the rooms here. But really they're nothing special." Her grin was unstoppable, filling her face with enthusiasm. She wore baggy denim jeans and her hair was pulled back in a long, blond braid.

"What if someone sees me?"

"I'll say you're my brother."

I couldn't help but laugh. "No way will ANYONE believe that!"

"Okay. You're my African-American cousin." She giggled. "My adopted cousin. But no one will see you anyway because I know a back way. Come with me."

So I followed around to the back of the property, into a small doorway, and then up ancient stairs that creaked and groaned with every footstep. There must have been a hundred of them. Finally, we stepped into a quiet hallway lined with many doors.

We stopped in front of one of these doors, then entered Allison's spacious room. It had green carpeting and two luxurious beds draped with yellow and green flowered bedspreads and matching throw pillows. A shelf with pictures, trophies, books, and potted plants lined one wall, while another wall had an ultramodern floor-to-ceiling entertainment center. There was also a large window, a private bathroom, and a walk-in closet that was larger than the bedroom I shared with my two brothers.

"Thought you said this was 'nothing special'!" I said, giving a low whistle.

"It's okay."

"Better than okay! I had no idea you lived like this. You made it sound like a dungeon, but this is great."

"It's nice—if you like rules, routine, and no privacy. My roommate Lucia is cool, but we have nothing in common. She's older and totally into this guy she's dating."

"It beats having TWO roommates."

"For sure. Still, I don't feel I belong here." She shoved her hands into her jeans pockets and made a face. "This room isn't ME. I liked staying at Varina's place better. Even with her uncle ill, I was comfortable there. It wasn't like the politically perfect house I grew up in or this structured prison. It was a REAL home."

"Like mine," I said wistfully, wondering if my house would ever be comfortable again—and realizing immediately that it wouldn't be until Kristyn returned. A lump clogged my throat. I glanced away, my gaze falling on the entertainment center. I spotted a dark, square object I hadn't noticed before.

"What are you staring at?" she asked.

"Allison, you never told me you had a laptop! I asked if you had an E-mail address and you said no."

"I don't do E-mail." She rolled her eyes. "My father sent the laptop as a reward for coming back to school and not telling the press about being illegally adopted. I'd have rather had a new tool belt. What am I going to do with a computer?"

"Everything!" I was already going over to the laptop, running my hand over it. "Let me show you."

"Whatever."

"You'll love this!" I assured her, delighted to find a modem attachment, which I plugged in.

I sensed Allison standing behind me as the computer came alive under my fingertips. My excitement, I reflected, must be similar to how a pianist might feel when performing at a concert. I entered some codes, heard an electronic clash of chords as I was connected on-line, then called up my E-mail.

"Watch this, Allison!" I exclaimed, pushing up my glasses as they slipped down my nose.

"What am I watching?" she asked skeptically.

"Cybermagic." I chuckled and pointed to the screen. "Your laptop is on-line and humming with info. See those messages? That's my E-mail."

"Your E-mail? Here?" She pulled up a chair and sat beside me. "But how can YOUR mail go to MY computer?"

"I connected to my server, keyed in some codes, and presto! Look—a message from Sam. I bet he found out more dirt on the Victors."

"Dr. Victor and Geneva?" I had Allison's full attention now. "And who's Sam?"

"A buddy of mine—a real hacker type. He found out where the Victors owned property, and I plan to check out an address near Monterey."

"Isn't that where Geneva bought those silver shoes you told me about?"

"Yeah. The police think the Victors are in Mexico, but I know it's not true. Sam sent me a picture of Geneva Victor, and it's definitely the same woman I saw at the inn."

"So let's go after the witch," Allison declared. "You can use your super vision to find her and then I'll use my strength to grab her and make her confess."

I shook my head. "Allison, you've been great, but I have to do this myself. It's my fault Kristyn is missing."

"It is NOT your fault. It's those creepy Victors. And I really want to help."

"So help me get to Monterey." I turned toward her. "You got a car?"

"Me? Not yet." She shook her head, her braid flopping from one shoulder to the other. "But I'm already hinting at one as a Christmas gift."

"How will I get to Monterey? Not another bus."

"No fear. My roommate has a car, and her boyfriend lives in Monterey. If I offer to pay for her gas, she'll take us. Both of us, Eric," she added firmly.

I frowned, hating to involve Allison any more than I had to. I didn't want to put her in danger. Still, I didn't have much choice.

"Okay," I finally agreed. "But once we reach the Victors' condo, I'm the one going in."

"We'll see" was all Allison would say, which didn't sound like a yes. But I wasn't in a position to argue.

I turned my attention back to the computer.

I quickly read my messages from Sam, who had found another medical article by Dr. Victor. This one was titled "Eugenics: Improving the Human Race."

"What's eugenics?" Allison asked, reading over my shoulder. "Some kind of diet plan?"

"A genetic diet for the human race. It's an article by Dr. Victor." I had begun reading and felt sick inside. "He wants to improve people by getting rid of imperfections."

"No way!" Allison cried, leaning closer to read the screen. I heard her give a soft gasp. "This is some kind of joke. No one really thinks like this. He can't be serious!"

"He is. He calls himself a visionary and vows to erase all human weaknesses. He plans to alter the genetic makeup of the future, and even mentions creating frozen clones for spare parts, like selling human organs at a mall."

"What if someone created US just for spare parts?" Allison asked with horror in her eyes. "I mean, we ARE clones. We don't know anything about who we were cloned from. If Varina's uncle and that woman doctor hadn't rescued us from that floating lab, what would have happened to us?"

"I don't know. But you know what's even creepier?"

"I'm afraid to ask. What?"

"When I first started surfing around the web to find more facts, I saw mostly just stuff about how humans share some DNA with bananas and how calves are being cloned with human genes. Then I found this site where people can sign up to be cloned at a foreign clinic."

"You're kidding!"

"Nope. It's a real website, but it might be a scam.

Still, it freaked me. I mean, how many more clones are out there? We know about you, me, Varina, Chase, and Sandee. But there could be MORE."

Allison looked at me intently. We didn't speak for a few minutes. Finally, she reached out and touched my hand. "Eric, did you really mean it?"

"What?" I asked solemnly.

"Do humans REALLY share DNA with bananas?"

The corners of her mouth twitched as she grinned. Then she laughed, and soon I was laughing so hard I could barely breathe.

We were still laughing when there was a sudden knock on the door and a gruff voice demanded, "Open up! Is there a BOY in the room?"

TWENTY-TWO

"Eric, hide!" Allison exclaimed. "You can't be found in here! Even I don't want to get in THAT much trouble!"

"But where? The closet?"

"No! That's the first place they'd look," Allison said in a low whisper. "Try under the bed."

The door rattled with pounding again.

I looked around, decided there wasn't enough room under the bed, and headed for the only other likely hiding place—the bathroom. I shut the door behind me, then crawled into the shower.

I heard the door open and then the chatter of excited voices. But I couldn't hear what was being said. Too bad I didn't have Chase's clone-enhanced hearing. Hmmm . . . but I did have a power of my own. I decided to test my own X-ray vision again.

So I took off my glasses and focused on the closed door.

Outside the voices dropped in tone and I swore I heard someone laughing. What was going on?

I concentrated as I stared, seeing past wood grain, to darkness, and then to bright shapes and colors. YES! I was seeing THROUGH the door, and this time I seemed more in control. Maybe it was only a matter of practice.

My gaze found Allison. She stood by one of the beds with a smile on her face and her arm stretched out as if she was pointing toward my hiding place. Then I saw the other person: a stocky olive-skinned girl a few years older than Allison with curly brown hair. They were both laughing.

Suddenly Allison's voice rang out loud and clear, "You can come out now, Eric!"

I stepped out of the shower, wiping my wet shoes on a rug. Then I cautiously peeked inside the room and whispered, "You sure?"

"Yeah." Allison came over to me. "I want you to meet my roommate, Lucia."

"Your roommate? Not a teacher?"

"Gotcha," Lucia said, giggling. "Can't believe you fell for that. All I did was lower my voice and sound tough."

"Lucia knew you were coming, and she has a sick sense of humor," Allison told me. "But since she's going to drive us to Monterey, we can forgive her."

"Please forgive me, Eric," Lucia said teasingly, setting down a heavy green backpack. "I don't usually make Allison's friends hide in the bathroom. At least not the cute ones."

Cute? I thought, embarrassed, and a little flattered. Then my manners kicked in and I nodded politely. "It's okay. Nice to meet you, Lucia."

"Oooh, what a great accent!" she exclaimed. "I just love southern accents."

"Texas," I said, even more embarrassed. "Uh, I'm from Marshall, Texas. You probably haven't heard of it."

"But I WANT to hear everything. My boyfriend used to live in Texas and I'll bet you'll just adore him. He's—"

Allison cut her off. "We can talk more later, Lucia. We really should leave."

"And you're going to pay for my whole tank of gas?" Lucia asked eagerly, reaching for a purse and pulling out a set of keys.

"You got it." Allison took her wallet from her pocket and waved a blue and gold credit card. "So let's get out of here before one of the teachers really DOES see Eric."

I stared curiously out the car windows, noting the bridges, heavily trafficked highways, miles of tall buildings, and glimpses of ocean. I'd often dreamed of traveling around the country, but figured it wouldn't happen till I finished high school. Yet here I was, riding in a cool, blue Corvette with two gorgeous girls. Wait till I told Marcos and Larry Joe!

Then I thought about Kristyn and felt guilty for having a good time. I couldn't forget her, not even for a minute.

We rode though a busy ribbon of road that curved through brown-green hills and flat farmland that stretched to the ocean. I'd never seen the Pacific Ocean before, and couldn't take my gaze away from the rolling, foaming waters that crashed into sand and jutting rocks. Awesome!

After we took an exit for Pacific Grove, Allison turned

to me. "Check the map for the street address."

"Okay." I unfolded the map and checked the street index. After I found the condo's address, I gave directions to Lucia.

"I know that area," Lucia said. "Not too far from where my sweetie lives. He's into kickboxing and seashell art. Eric, you want to stop at his place first so you guys can meet?"

"Maybe another time," I answered.

"Your loss," she said with a shrug.

"Finding my sister is really important," I said grimly, glancing at the passing houses, apartments, and businesses, wondering if I was getting closer to Kristyn.

"This is it!" Allison exclaimed, pointing toward a sprawling dark-shingled navy-blue and beige building. "It's the condo with the wrought-iron fence. You can drop us off here, Lucia."

"Want me to wait for you?" Lucia asked as the car slowed to a stop.

"Don't bother," Allison said. "This could take a few minutes or a few hours. We'll call you when we're ready to leave."

"Suit yourself." Lucia shrugged. "I hope you guys know what you're doing."

"So do we," I said grimly. Then Allison and I waved as Lucia drove away.

A stiff salty breeze slapped against my skin, and I rubbed my chilled arms. Glancing up at the sky, I saw that heavy gray clouds had covered the sun, stealing the warmth and showering the air with cool mist. I shivered.

"Remember, I'm the one going in," I told Allison, trying to sound tough and confident. "You'll wait outside."

"Don't pull that macho stuff."

"Kristyn is MY sister."

"And I'm your friend. We should work together."

"So I'll work on the inside, and you'll keep watch on the outside."

"You better not order me around," she warned. "I could pick you up like you weigh nothing."

"You wouldn't!" Standing beside a towering palm tree, I suddenly felt very small.

"I WOULD." There was a gleam in her eyes that I did NOT like. I'd already seen how she could lift more than triple her own weight.

"You're not the only one with unusual powers," I retorted. "With my vision, I could look at you, I mean, look through your—" I hesitated, my cheeks suddenly warm. "Anyway, I could see more than you'd want me to see."

"You wouldn't!" she exclaimed.

"I WOULD."

"Checkmate!" Allison rang out.

We both laughed, then suddenly Allison's gaze softened and she gently reached out to touch my hand. "Hey, I know you're worried about your sister. I want to find her, too."

"I appreciate that."

"So go ahead, storm the building, Mr. Macho. I'll wait here."

"Thanks," I said quietly, with an anxious look at the seemingly quiet condo.

Then I hesitated. Now what? I'd crossed several states to get here, but I couldn't just go to the door, knock, and demand the safe return of my sister. What was the best plan? Sneak around the building and look for an unlocked door or opened window?

"You going or what?" Allison asked, tightening her jacket as an ocean breeze picked up.

"I'm going. I'm just trying to figure things out. If Kristyn's being held there, I have to be careful or she could get hurt." I pursed my lips, frustrated because no great ideas were coming to me. If only I knew what was going on inside the condo. But maybe there was a way to find out. . . .

I reached for my glasses, took them off, and handed them to Allison.

"Cool!" she cried. "You're gonna use your super sight."

"I'll try, but I can't always control it," I admitted. The dizziness began hitting me hard and the world started swaying and tilting. Everything blurred, and if I hadn't been leaning against the palm tree, I might have fallen over. I heard Allison ask if I was okay, but I just nodded and concentrated on my vision.

Colors blended like a melting rainbow, curving and stretching in all directions. Then the colors fused together and shapes became solid images. Dark wood grains changed to a blinding burst of white—white walls, carpets, and furniture.

"I'm IN," I murmured to Allison.

"Do you see anyone?" I heard her ask.

"Not yet." Talking took too much energy, so I shut out Allison and slipped deeper into the condo. To the right I saw pale counters, a sink, a refrigerator—the kitchen. Still no sign of life. The only movement was a dripping faucet.

Then I caught a whirl of dark movement. Sweat dripped down my brow and I felt as if my head was going to explode. Every cell in my body screamed for me to quit, to get out, but I couldn't stop now.

So I shut out the world and stared where I'd seen the dark movement. There it was again, something as black as danger and as alive as fear. Bristly charcoal-black fur, jagged white teeth, and fiery yellow eyes that could burn through the sun.

A wolf.

TWENTY-THREE

"Eric! Come out of it!" Allison's voice drifted through my foggy, fear-shocked brain.

All I could see were snarling jaws and evil eyes, as if I were being sucked into some weird trap. I knew I was standing outside in the salty chilled air, yet part of me was inside—with the wolf.

Suddenly Allison grabbed me, yelled something, and pushed my glasses back over my eyes.

"What?" I blinked and shook my head. "Did you see it? The wolf?"

"Wolf?" Her dark eyes were wide with disbelief. "No way!"

"But I saw one—a huge, dark hairy beast with teeth that could make bubble gum out of a shark." I knew I was talking fast, trying to hide my nervousness. I loved dogs, but I'd seen wolves lurking outside our ranch and knew well enough to fear them.

"Incredible!" Allison said, staring with awe across the street. "Talk about a watchdog. Whoever lives there must REALLY have something to hide."

"Like a kidnapped girl," I said grimly. Then, even though a part of me wanted to run miles away from that wolf, I crossed my arms over my chest and pursed my lips. "I'm going around back and try to get inside."

"Not alone you aren't."

"It's safer if you keep a lookout here."

"I'm not falling for that." She stood tall and set her expression in cemented determination. "Besides, how do you expect to climb over that large wall without my help?"

I looked at the thick adobe-style restraining wall that encircled the small condo. The wall was at least eight feet high, as smooth and as slick as a waterslide. There was a wrought-iron gate with sharp spikes that spread across the top.

I sighed and muttered, "Okay." Then we crossed the street and cautiously approached a tree-shaded corner of the wall. Glancing around to make sure no one was watching, Allison lifted herself to the top and reached down to swing me up beside her; then we both jumped down to the gravel path on the other side.

"There's a window," Allison said, pointing to the back of the house, which dipped into a patio where baskets and pots of greenery decorated a cozy enclosed area.

Allison was already climbing onto a brick planter to peek into the window. I came up beside her. "You see anything yet?"

"Yeah," she replied, her voice rising with excitement. "It's a back bedroom and the door's open, so I can see into another room. Something is moving!"

"The wolf?"

"I—I don't know. . . . It's dark gray and—" Suddenly she broke off and started laughing, and not so quietly, either.

"Shhsh!" I warned, putting my finger to my lips. "What if someone is inside? They'll hear you!"

But she kept laughing, which really annoyed me. This was a serious situation.

Gritting my teeth, I stepped up beside her and peered into the room, my glasses clinking when they touched the windowpane. And I saw something move . . . something black, furry, and SMALL.

"Eric!" Allison hiccuped, she was laughing so hard. "Your wolf isn't a giant beast."

"It's not?"

"No!" More laughter. "Only a tiny terrier. Like Toto in *The Wizard of Oz*."

I blinked, totally humiliated. Not a large, monster dog, but a fuzzy toy-sized terrier. And yet when I'd peered inside the house, the dog seemed enormous. A snarling, vicious monster. How had I been so wrong?

Finally Allison stopped laughing, and apologized. "Sorry, but it is funny."

"Maybe to you," I muttered, frustrated at not being more skilled with my vision. Couldn't I do anything right?

"We all make mistakes. Don't take it so hard, Eric." Allison reached out and gave my hand a reassuring squeeze. "I'm just glad you *were* wrong."

"Well, yeah. But little dogs can bite hard, too."

"Let's just figure out a way inside."

"You're strong," I said, with an edge of envy. "Rip the door off."

"I'm not ripping anything unless I know your sister

is inside. Use your super eyes again, and check out the whole house this time."

"Why bother? I'll just mess up."

"No you won't. Give it a try."

Frowning, but encouraged by her confidence in me, I took off my glasses. Dizziness, and then clarity. Okay, I could do this. I focused on each room in the condo: kitchen, living room, bathrooms, two bedrooms, and even the closets. Not one single person—only the small fuzzy dog, who was harmlessly curled up in a doggy bed.

"Darn." Disappointment hit me hard. "Kristyn's not in there."

A short time later, Lucia arrived to pick us up. She asked questions, but Allison and I gave only vague answers. I was grateful Allison didn't make jokes about the "monster" wolf.

Instead, she suggested I stay the night in Monterey with Lucia's "sweetie" rather than risk being caught in an all-girls school. Tomorrow Allison would return and we'd figure out a new plan.

"Sweetie" was Darzell, a cool guy who talked about growing up in Texas, showed me some of his driftwood art, then spent the rest of the evening teaching me kickboxing moves. I wasn't coordinated enough to copy the moves, but I got a few good kicks in before Darzell knocked me flat on my rear. He thought this was a hoot, while I rubbed my backside and wobbled to my feet.

Before I went to bed, I debated whether or not to call my family. Dad would probably just yell at me some more. And since the news reported my sister as still missing, Mom would be so distraught it wouldn't be any easier to talk to her.

In the end, I decided to wait another day to call. Perhaps tomorrow would bring some answers and renewed hope.

But the morning dawned and I didn't have any new ideas for finding my sister. Waiting around for Allison and Lucia to show up was frustrating. I jumped every time the phone rang or a car drove by.

At noon, Allison and Lucia showed up—with one other person.

I stared in surprise at the slender, auburn-haired girl who stood beside Allison: a girl who, like me, had been cloned secretly fifteen years ago and possessed unusual powers.

I smiled at the "clone cousin" I had met only once before and greeted Varina.

TWENTY-FOUR

Los Angeles, CA

"You're looking for Sandee Yoon?" Serena gasped.

"I am," the blond guy said, sounding hopeful. "Do you know her?"

Serena stared, shocked that he didn't realize who she was. Of course, since leaving home she had drastically changed her appearance. Her short blond-streaked black hair, bright mauve lipstick, heavy mascara, and punk-style clothes gave her a mature, edgy look. Not even Amishka knew she was only fifteen. And she never got carded anymore, which was so cool.

"Do I know Sandee?" Serena repeated, giving herself time to think. "Well . . . maybe I do and maybe I don't. Why?"

"I'm worried about her," he said with a frown, running his rugged hand over his forehead. His snug navy-blue jeans and light blue shirt were rumpled, as if he'd been sleeping in them, and the dark bags under his eyes contrasted with his very blond hair.

"Worried?" Serena scoffed. "Yeah, right."

"Really. It's urgent I find her." He spoke sincerely, and her skin chilled. Who was this guy, anyway? A hunk, for sure. But she'd never seen him before, so what was his game?

"I'd like to help you, only I've kind of got my own problem here. I shouldn't just be standing around—" She heard the ding of the elevator and glanced over her shoulder anxiously, but when two kids and their parents alighted, she relaxed a little. Maybe Ravage had stopped looking for her.

"I can see you're stressed over something." Concern flared on his face. "Can I help?"

"No. I just need to talk to some friends."

"Fever Pitch, right?"

She nodded, still suspicious, but felt completely pulled into his gray-blue gaze. She was used to roadies and totally scummy guys who hit on her like it was a sport and she was the prize. But this guy was different. . . .

"What's your name?" she asked.

"Chase Rinaldi. And yours?"

"Serena." She flashed her practiced "sparkling" smile, the one that usually suckered guys in like a siren's call.

"Just Serena?"

"Right. Like Madonna. Cher. Brandy. I'm gonna be this major singer when I get my chance. And maybe I CAN tell you something about Sandee. Now just isn't a good time."

"Name the time and the place, and I'll be there."

"Good answer," she said approvingly.

"So this is a test?" He chuckled. "Did I pass?"

"The scores aren't in yet."

"Anyway, I gotta find Sandee, to make sure she's okay. It's important and time's running out. Can you help me or not?"

"I can help, only I'm not gonna tell a total stranger where my friend is unless I know I can trust you."

"I'm not asking for trust, only information."

"So meet me tomorrow morning at ten in the coffee shop by the lobby." She glanced uneasily up and down the hall. "And don't bother quizzing Fever Pitch. None of them knew Sandee, not the way I did. If I decide to trust you, I can tell you where she is."

"Fair enough." He nodded, easing into a faint smile. "See you in the morning, Serena."

"Yeah." She met his smile and held on to it for a mesmerizing moment. "See you then, Chase."

TWENTY-FIVE

Varina had a way of looking at a person and really hearing what they were saying.

"Don't worry, Eric. We'll find your sister," Varina assured me from across Darzell's couch. Lucia and her boyfriend had gone off somewhere, and told us we could hang out until they returned.

"But where can we look for her?" I asked. "I was so sure she'd be in that condo."

"What about other property the Victors own?" Allison asked, reaching into a bag of Doritos and grabbing a handful. She held out the bag to me, but I shook my head.

"There's acreage in Red Bluff and an apartment in San Jose," I answered. "If I had my E-mail, I could tell you the other investment property—a few are even in other countries." My heart lurched with quick alarm. "Do you think they took Kristyn to another country? The police said Dr. Victor and Geneva were in Mexico."

"But you know that can't be true. You saw her," Varina pointed out.

"Yeah. She really did look like a sweet old granny. She had me fooled."

"Geneva fooled me once, too," Varina admitted. "Luckily Chase helped me realize what a fake she was."

"Speaking of Chase . . ." Allison leaned closer to Varina and flashed a mischievous smile. "Any news of him?"

"Yeah. He calls me sometimes." Her cheeks reddened and she spoke softly. "He found Fever Pitch in Los Angeles, so he's really hoping to find Sandee Yoon. After that, he'll return home."

"That's great!" I told her.

"But where is Chase's home?" Allison's blond brows arched with purpose. "Is he going to move back to Reno?"

"Not Reno. With his parents and house gone, there's nothing there for him. But—" Varina glanced down at her clenched hands, her cheeks growing redder. "But Uncle Jim told Chase he'd always have a home with us. He invited Chase to stay. And we're really hoping he will."

"Then he'd be like your stepbrother," Allison teased.

"NOT EVEN!" Varina snapped, then covered her mouth with quick embarrassment. "I mean, he may have pretended to be my stepbrother to save me from going into a foster home when Uncle Jim was in the hospital, but Chase and I are definitely NOT related."

"How can you be sure?" I asked. "None of us know who we were cloned from."

"Except for—" Varina bit her lip and glanced away.

"I just know Chase and I don't share the same DNA, so there's no way we can be related."

"Good thing, too—FOR YOU," Allison said with a wicked grin, which caused Varina to blush the deepest shade of red I'd ever seen. That's when I realized what was going on. Varina liked Chase, and not in a sisterly way. But she seemed kind of young for an intense guy like Chase. And I wondered if Chase returned her feelings.

"Let's just figure out how to help Kristyn," Varina said sharply. She pursed her lips and thoughtfully gazed out a window that offered a distant glimpse of blue ocean. "We know Geneva has Kristyn, so all we have to do is find Geneva. She may be able to disguise herself cleverly, but there are some things even Geneva can't hide."

"Like what?" I asked.

"Her greedy habits. She's the type to stay in luxurious hotels near ritzy shopping centers. She'd go somewhere comfortable, and yet someplace no one would look for her."

"The police think the fake Eleanor Corvit went to New York," I said bitterly. "They fell for her disguise."

"But we know the truth," Allison said, reaching out to squeeze my hand.

"Corvit. That name . . ." Varina suddenly furrowed her brow and asked, "Was it spelled C-O-R-V-I-T?"

"Yeah." I nodded. "Why?"

"I've always been good at puzzles and word games—especially anagrams." Varina curled up her legs on the striped blue and white couch beneath her. " 'Corvit' is an anagram."

"I know!" Allison waved a Dorito in the air. "For Victor. 'Corvit' and 'Victor' have the same letters."

"You're right!" I hit my hand to my forehead and groaned at my own denseness. I'd never been good at that kind of thing.

"Eric, you've uncovered plenty of other useful information," Varina said as if reading my thoughts. "I bet if we analyze the information, we may discover something important."

"I could write down a list of the things I've learned so far," I offered.

"Don't bother." Allison nudged me. "Lists aren't necessary with Varina around. Just tell her. She can memorize anything."

"It's not always a good thing. Believe me, you wouldn't enjoy remembering everything from our past." Varina tapped her fingers on the table and frowned. "Like the night Dr. Hart and Uncle Jim helped us escape. It's terrible to replay the moment Dr. Victor shot Dr. Hart over and over in my mind. I—I wish I knew if she survived."

"You never found out what happened to her?" I asked.

"No. Although I have odd memories of a woman with long red hair trying to comfort me. And sometimes I have nightmares where I hear Dr. Hart's screams and see blood spreading on her chest . . ."

"So she probably died," Allison guessed.

"I don't know. I'm not so sure." Varina shook her head, a wisp of auburn hair sweeping across her brow. "Uncle Jim is a lot better, but when I ask about my past, his head hurts and he almost has a panic attack. So I stopped asking." She shrugged, but I could tell this was an upsetting topic. "Besides, I've pieced together a lot from my own memories. After we find Kristyn, I'll tell you more."

"You'd better," Allison said. "I don't like all these

mysteries. And I have so many questions about our birth, the freaky powers, and who we were cloned from."

"Me, too," I admitted, wondering if there was a grown-up Eric out there somewhere—or even weirder, an exact double of me. But I pushed these thoughts aside and added, "Right now all I care about is finding Kristyn."

"I understand." Varina nodded sympathetically. Then she asked me to tell her everything I knew about my sister's disappearance: how "Mrs. Corvit" and "Mitch" had pretended to be from a TV show, the things I'd overheard while hiding under the bed, and the other information I'd gotten from cyberspace.

When I'd finished, Varina stared out the window for a long time, and I could tell her computer-like brain was in "search" mode. Still, I was startled after a long moment of silence when she suddenly snapped her fingers and exclaimed, "That's it!"

"WHAT?" Allison and I both asked.

"I know where we should search next." Her green eyes lit up with excitement. "You said it yourself, Eric."

"I did?"

"Yeah. Geneva Victor is into possessions and can't resist shopping. And she LOVES shoes. . . ."

The meaning of Varina's words suddenly hit me. "The silver shoes!"

"Right," she said, smiling at me.

Allison looked at Varina and then at me, shaking her blond head in perplexity. "What are you two talking about?"

"We're back on Geneva's trail, that's what." I grabbed Allison's hand and pulled her off the couch. "Come on! Let's go check out Pacific Soles!"

TWENTY-SIX

We found a phone book and located Pacific Soles Shoe Boutique—which turned out to be less than two miles away. Since we didn't have a car, we started walking.

Gray clouds billowed in from the ocean, but bright rays of sun broke through. We found a paved bicycle/walking trail and moved briskly, with the sound of crashing waves and refreshing salty ocean breezes swirling around us. If it hadn't been for my terrible fears for Kristyn, I might have enjoyed myself.

Kristyn had now been gone over three days. I'd checked the news a few times, but there were no new leads or breakthroughs. Mitch and his "elderly companion" had escaped so completely, it was as if they'd vanished into another dimension. And the police sounded doubtful about Kristyn's safe return. They uttered horrid phrases like "suspected foul play," then showed a smiling photo of a dark-haired young woman: Mitch's last victim. I felt sick to my stomach just thinking about it. Too much time had passed since Kristyn's kidnapping; too many horrible things could have happened.

Was my sister afraid?

Was she in pain?

Was she alive?

She just HAD to be alive. I wouldn't give up looking till I found her. And I was getting closer. I could feel it.

"There's Pacific Soles." Allison, who had automatically assumed the role of group leader, pointed toward a small row of shops on a side street.

Pacific Soles fit snugly between an art shop and a gourmet candy store. Elegant rows of shoes were displayed on glass pedestals in an expansive front window.

Allison stopped suddenly, turning to Varina with her hand held out. "Before we go in, I'll have to do some repair work. Do you have any makeup with you?"

"Some," Varina replied, opening her purse. "Santa Monica Mauve Frost lipstick, mascara, and a choice of Jade Jewel, Silver Mist, and Perilous Pink eye shadows."

"Great!" Allison walked over to a parked car, then used the side-view mirror to sweep on painted hues with the skill of an artist creating a masterpiece. She grabbed an edge of her baggy yellow cotton shirt and twisted it into a knot so that it hugged her narrow hips. For the final touch, she reached up and unraveled her long braid, letting loose a golden waterfall of hair.

"So what do you think?" Allison asked with a mischievous grin. "Do I look like a girl now?"

"That's an understatement," Varina teased, giving a

low whistle. "I'm hiding my makeup from you when Chase comes back."

"You look good," I said simply, with some embarrassment.

Then Allison led the way to Pacific Soles. As we walked inside and onto the thick beige carpet, a bell signaled our arrival.

Immediately a woman stepped toward us. She wore a light pink suit, matching low-heeled shoes, and a rounded white hat on her frosted blue-gray cap of hair. She oozed sophistication, and a glance at my rumpled jeans and faded T-shirt made me wonder if I should have waited outside.

Allison smiled graciously and extended her hand to the woman. "Good afternoon. What a charming place you have here."

"Thank you." After a brisk handshake, the woman's gaze held Allison's as if they shared a common language. "I'm Ellen Carrouthers. How may I help you?"

Allison pointed to a display of spiked heels and smoothly launched into a story about needing a pair of shoes for an upcoming "debutante cotillion"—whatever that was! I glanced over at Varina and exchanged a smile. When she nodded, I nodded back: our signal to get to work.

I casually browsed around the shop, which was small and yet crammed full of thousands of shoes. It didn't take long to find what I was looking for: a pair of silver shoes that were identical to the ones from Geneva's suitcase.

I tapped Varina on the shoulder and pointed at the shoes.

"The same ones?" she whispered.

"Yeah. Including the high price tag."

"Too rich for me. But totally Geneva."

Allison was still talking to the store clerk. I managed to catch her eye and nod toward the silver shoes. As we'd already arranged, Allison then swept over to where we stood and gave a delighted squeal. "Oh! Look at those silver darlings! Exactly like the ones my dear friend Mrs. Victor owns."

"You know Geneva Victor?" Ms. Carrouthers asked, showing quick interest.

"Oh, yes. Doesn't everyone?" Allison gave this brittle kind of phony laugh. "Although I haven't seen dear Geneva in ages. Oh! It would be such a lark to get together with her. I haven't the faintest idea where she's wintering this season. I'd heard she was in Mexico."

"Perhaps she was, but no longer. She was here yesterday. You JUST missed her," the clerk said with a slight lift of her brows.

"She was here!" Allison didn't hide her excitement.

"Oh, yes. She was replacing those very silver shoes, apparently she'd lost one, and wanted them for the upcoming La Brenz art exhibit she's sponsoring."

"That is just so fab! I'll call her . . . only I don't have her address or number."

"That IS too bad," Mrs. Carrouthers said with a nod. "I do wish I could help you, but I'm not allowed to give out our customers' personal information."

"Not even to their DEAREST friends?" Allison asked with a pout. "Geneva will be devastated if she finds out I tried to contact her and failed."

"I am sorry, but rules are rules." Mrs. Carrouthers pursed her lips firmly.

"Is she staying at the beach condo?" Allison persisted.

"I don't think so, although I really can't say more on the subject." The clerk smiled. "Would you like to try on these shoes? Silver is such a lovely shade for your coloring."

I watched disappointment cross Allison's face, but I had to give her credit for keeping up her act. She told the clerk that she would indeed love to try on the shoes, but her size—a 7½ triple A—might be hard to fit.

"No problem," the clerk replied smoothly. "I'll simply check in the back. Please excuse me for a moment."

As soon as she disappeared into the back room, Allison faced Varina and me. "We don't have much time. Any ideas?"

"If you distract Mrs. Carrouthers, Eric and I could check her files." Varina pointed to a tall metal filing cabinet in a far corner of the store.

"The files are probably locked," Allison pointed out. "Besides, we'd never get near them without being noticed."

"I don't have to be near the files to read them," I said.

Varina arched her brows. "What do you mean?"

"It'll take some concentration, but I think I can see into the filing cabinet." I tried to sound confident, although I couldn't forget my "wolf" mistake.

"Cool!" Varina exclaimed.

Allison nodded her approval. "Great idea, Eric."

"Let's see if it works first. I'll need a paper and pen to write the information down."

"I can be your notebook," Varina offered with a shy smile. "Whisper the information to me, and I'll remember it."

"Do you ever forget anything?" I asked.

"Sure. I'm still figuring out my powers."

"Yeah. I know what you mean." My glasses were slipping down my nose, so I reached up to push them in place. "Only I seem to mess up all the time."

"I mess up, too, mostly when I'm remembering things. Strong emotions get in the way. And sometimes I can't tell the difference between what's happening now and what's already happened."

Just then Mrs. Carrouthers returned holding three shoe boxes, which she proudly offered to Allison.

With the clerk's focus on Allison, I moved closer to the file cabinets and lifted off my glasses. Okay, here goes nothing, I thought. I crossed my fingers and hoped my powers wouldn't fail me this time.

I stared at the metal drawer labeled "R–Z." The dizziness hit as hard as usual, but Varina put her hand on my shoulder to steady me. Focus, Eric, I ordered myself. I saw gray metal, then rows of white papers. The white papers came closer until I could read the typed words. Names raced across the tops of the folders: Rapp, Sweeny, Swinehart, Smithee, Trent, Ullrich, Victor—

YES! Found it! I concentrated deeply on the Victor file. It was a thick folder with many yellow slips of paper that I guessed were copies of sales receipts. I zoomed closer, searching for an address or phone number. I found Geneva's name, then a line for an address, but it was only a post office box—just like what I'd read on her driver's license.

"You find it yet?" I heard Varina whisper.

"Only a post office box. . . . But here's something else."

"What?"

"A phone number with a 408 area code." I quickly told it to her, then put my glasses back on.

"That's in San Jose."

"Need me to repeat it?"

"No. I got it. Watch out!" Varina exclaimed as she grabbed my arm. "The clerk and Allison are coming over!"

TWENTY-SEVEN

"They are all so lovely! I can't decide which pair I like best," Allison said graciously as the clerk led her toward a nearby shoe display.

"What about these charming suede pumps?" Mrs. Carrouthers gestured to a pair of rust-colored shoes, giving Varina and me a curious sideways glance. But we were simply standing there doing nothing, so the clerk returned her full attention to Allison.

"Would you like to try these on?" the clerk asked.

"I don't know." Allison picked up one rust-colored shoe, studied it for a moment, then set it back down.

Varina stepped over to Allison, shaking her head. "No, Allison. Those shoes are not your style."

"I know, but they're so fab. It's just so hard to make up my mind." Allison twisted her lips into an elegant pout. "I suppose I'll have to think it over and come back another day."

Mrs. Carrouthers heard this and was clearly disappointed, but I was just grateful for the smooth exit out of the store.

"That's SO cool you got Geneva's phone number," Allison told me, carefully stepping over a jagged chunk of sidewalk. "Good going, Eric."

"Thanks." I pointed across the busy narrow street. "There's a pay phone."

We waited for a stoplight, then walked over to the public phone. The directory was missing and the clear booth walls were plastered with a collage of flyers and graffiti.

"I'm not good on the phone," I said. "Allison should make the call."

"Yeah," Varina agreed, pushing back her loose auburn curls. "Go for it, Al. If Geneva answers, she won't recognize your voice. You can pretend to be selling something."

"Clones for sale?" she teased.

"Got any spare parts?" I chuckled.

"Cut it out, you guys!" Varina shuddered. "Being a clone is NOT a joke. I don't know how you can laugh about it."

"Most famous comedians are crying on the inside," I pointed out. "Laughter makes you feel better. We can't change what we are, so we might as well make the best of it."

"Yeah," Allison agreed, twisting her long blond hair into a braid as she walked, then wiping off the lipstick with a tissue from her pocket. "It's cool being strong. But the best thing about being a clone is finding you guys."

"I guess you're right." Varina smiled. "I'm glad I have you guys."

"Me, too," Allison said. "And since my family sucks big-time, it means twice as much to have friends like you."

"Good friends aren't easy to come by," I said. I glanced at the phone. "Will you make the call, Allison?"

"Sure. What should I say?"

"Make up something. You were great with that snooty clerk," Varina said. "You'll think of a clever story."

"I'll do my best." Allison reached for the phone and keyed in a series of numbers, probably including her own calling card.

"It's ringing!" she said excitedly. "One, two . . . and . . . Hello, this is Alicia Stonesilver from the Eternal Rest Funeral Home. . . . Oh, yes, I mean sí. Uh . . . *habla*, uh, Señora Victor?" Allison covered the phone with her hand. "I think this is the housekeeper. Anyone know Spanish?"

"Taco and enchilada?" Varina shook her head. "Not me."

"I had two years of Spanish at school," I admitted. Then, uneasily, I took the receiver. *"Con quién habla? Dónde está Señora Victor?"* I listened to the soft, rapid Spanish of a woman who was named Consuela, but my Spanish wasn't good enough to catch more than a few phrases. When I asked to speak to the Victors, I was told, *"No está aquí. Ellos fueren a su casa en Cabo San Lucas."* Easy enough to figure out.

Disappointed, I hung up the phone. "Their housekeeper says they're at their home in Cabo San Lucas."

"Mexico?" Varina asked.

"Yeah. It's SO frustrating." I clenched my hands, fighting a strong urge to pound something. "Another dead end."

"Don't worry, Eric." Varina gave me a sympathetic look. "We'll keep trying."

"But all the clues are going nowhere. I know Geneva Victor is somewhere around here. I have to find my sister. I'd really hoped to call my parents with good news today."

"Calling them is a good idea," Varina suggested. "Let them know you're still searching. It'll make them feel better, and you, too."

I rubbed my head and then blew out a deep, weary breath of air. "You think so?"

"Yeah," Varina said, and Allison nodded her agreement.

So I reached for the phone and dialed. Remembering my last talk with Dad, I tensed, afraid of more yelling and arguing. But when Dad answered, he sounded so relieved and happy to hear from me that I actually got choked up.

"Eric! Are you all right?"

"Yeah. But—but I haven't found her." My voice broke a little. "I've tried, Dad, really I have. But nothing's working right. I'm sorry."

"There's nothing to be sorry about, son," Dad said huskily. "You've done good. But there's no need to search for your sister in California. You should come home."

"Why?" My heart jumped. "What's happened?"

"We've had news." Dad's voice came through strong and hopeful. "Eric, we've heard from Kristyn."

TWENTY-EIGHT

Los Angeles, CA

As Serena hurried to the coffee shop, her footsteps clip-clopped an exciting beat. She couldn't wait to tell someone her news. BIG FANTABULOUS NEWS! She could barely hold herself together, she was so energized and jazzed.

In the coffee shop, she saw the blond guy, Chase Rinaldi, right away. Against her better judgment, she felt a buzz of attraction. He was even better-looking than she remembered. She kind of wished she didn't have to lie to him.

At least she could tell him a few truths, beginning with the news she'd just gotten from Slam.

"Guess what?" she announced, sweeping into a chair beside Chase and skipping the usual greetings.

"You found Sandee Yoon?"

"No!" She dismissed the question with a wave of her hand. "Sandee is old news—this is NEW and THRILLING. And I just have to tell someone."

"Is that supposed to make me feel flattered?" he replied in a light, bantering tone.

" 'Honored' would be a better word," she tossed back, unable to resist a flirtatious flutter of her eyes and a lift of her brows.

"Should I order something to eat first?"

"My news can't wait!"

"Go ahead." He smiled. "Fire away."

"Last night after the show, Slam listened to me sing. I mean, really listened! He said I had star quality, that he was going to arrange for me to record a song, get an agent, and talk to some big people in the business!"

Her head was spinning. After all this time, after wanting and yearning for so much so badly, it was really going to happen.

"Guess I should get your autograph now, before you're a big star," Chase teased. "Congratulations, Serena."

"Thanks! Only I can't stay for breakfast. I have to get ready, and then Slam's taking me to the record studio!"

"But you haven't told me about Sandee."

"Oh. Her." Serena found herself oddly jealous of her former identity, and she was suddenly VERY curious about why Chase was looking for her. Glancing at her watch, she decided to stay a few minutes longer.

"What's the deal with Sandee?" she asked, tucking her feet under her chair and hearing a soft clink as her ankle band brushed a chair leg.

"I need to speak to Sandee directly," Chase said. "Just tell me where she is."

"Uh . . . she moved on to a new gig. Yeah, she met

this drummer and took off with his group. I think she's hanging out in Sacramento now."

"What group?" he asked eagerly.

"First tell me the reason. You seem like an okay guy, but how do I know you're not a sicko or pervert?"

"You don't. I'm asking you to trust me." His light eyes darkened, causing her to shiver. Wow, this guy sure ran deep. She was intrigued.

Still, no way was she going to tell him she was Sandee. Serena was the rising star, Sandee was the loser.

"Sandee is with a group called the Tyrants," Serena lied. "If I hear from her, I'll give her a message."

"I either talk to her in person or not at all."

"She probably won't even want to talk to you."

"She will when I explain things. I know secrets about her birth, before she went into foster care. Tell her that, and ask her to call me on my cell phone."

"YOU KNOW ABOUT HER BIRTH?" Serena nearly fell off her chair.

"I know a lot." He met her gaze and held it tight. "Do you remember if Sandee has a strange tattoo on her ankle?"

Serena almost gasped. To cover her shock, she said quickly, "Uh, yeah. She has these tiny numbers on her ankle. She even asked me to make her a silver ankle band like mine to hide the tattoo. She never takes it off."

"Makes sense." Chase nodded. "I have a tattoo like that on my ankle. Does Sandee have any unusual . . . skills?"

"Like what?" Serena asked, then glanced over to the hotel lobby, where she saw a familiar face. "OH, LOOK! There's Slam! He's the one I told you about."

Chase turned, tilting his head to one side. "That tall guy with the nose ring and mustache?"

"Yeah. Although I don't know the long-haired guy he's with."

"That's odd, because they're talking about YOU."

"They are?" Serena peered at the two men conversing in the hotel lobby—more than fifty feet away. "But how can you know that? Do you lip-read or something?"

"Or something. Slam just said, 'It's all set with Serena.' "

"Oooh! Maybe the long-haired guy works for a record label!" Serena exclaimed. "What else are they saying?"

Chase stared at the men, tilting his head as if he could actually hear what they were saying—which of course, Serena told herself, was impossible. She waited for him to tell her more, but suddenly he scowled and grabbed her arm. "Come on, Serena."

"What's wrong?"

"You're getting out of here," he said roughly. "Slam is bad news."

"He is NOT! He's going to make me a star!"

"I don't think so."

"But Slam promised to get me a recording contract with a big-name studio."

"He's working on a contract all right, only not the kind you want."

"What's that supposed to mean?"

"Slam is NOT your friend. He just paid that long-haired guy to take care of you. Permanently." Chase's voice dropped to a whisper. "Your friend Slam wants you DEAD."

TWENTY-NINE

"Y ou've heard from Kristyn?" I asked my father, gripping the phone more tightly.

"Yes, Eric," Dad replied. "Kristyn called her friend Robin last night. Kristyn told Robin she'd met a young man over the Internet and ran away to meet him."

"IMPOSSIBLE!" I exclaimed, torn between outrage and relief. "Kristyn doesn't even have her own E-mail address. She always uses mine when she wants to surf the web."

"That's why the police are having an expert check out your computer."

"MY COMPUTER! You let them take my computer!"

"Eric, they won't damage it." Dad sounded weary. "And Kristyn is still missing. Finding her is all that matters right now. She wouldn't tell Robin where she was. She would only say she's with a friend and she'll come home when she's ready."

"No way! That doesn't sound like Kristyn."

"Your mother and I find it hard to swallow, too." Dad added quietly, "Eric, you need to come back home. I'll arrange for your airline ticket."

"Okay, Dad." We discussed details, then I hung up the phone. When I turned around, I found Allison and Varina staring at me.

"Is Kristyn okay?" Allison asked eagerly.

"I guess so. She called her best friend and said she was fine." I quickly relayed what Dad told me, mentally sorting things out and trying to make sense of them.

Robin wouldn't be fooled by someone impersonating Kristyn's voice, I reasoned, so Kristyn must be all right. But why call Robin and not our house? Of course, the phone lines at home were probably tapped. Maybe Kristyn figured as much and didn't want to be found.

Still, I couldn't buy the story of my sister running off to meet some strange guy. Kristyn could be impulsive and a real pain, but she was NEVER sneaky or dishonest. And why leave BEFORE her exciting parade performance, not AFTERWARD?

Totally confusing.

"I need to get to the San Francisco airport," I told my friends. "It's obvious that I'm not helping my family by being here. I might as well leave."

"Give up, you mean?" Varina accused.

"Leaving is NOT giving up." Her words hurt like a punch in the gut. "Just because Geneva Victor was at my house posing as an old lady doesn't mean she and Mitch kidnapped my sister. Maybe Kristyn really is with an E-mail friend. Coming out here was a waste of everyone's time, including my own."

"Eric, you're wrong." Allison shook her blond head.

"Trying to help someone else is NEVER a waste of time."

Varina nodded, rubbing her chin thoughtfully. "Besides, I have a bad feeling about Kristyn. I think she's still in danger."

I shivered at these words, knowing Varina had been cloned with keen mental abilities. Her "bad feelings" were nothing to be ignored.

The three of us stood awkwardly on the sidewalk while traffic passed by. No one said anything for a while. The sun had burst out in full force and droves of carefree people were heading for the beach and boardwalk. I wished I were on a family vacation, and that Kristyn were here with me.

But wishing it wasn't going to make it happen.

And standing around here wasn't bringing me any closer to finding my sister. The best move was to head home.

"This whole trip has been a failure. Leave it to Eric the Klutz to screw up again," I said bitterly. Frustrated, I slapped my hand against one of the walls shielding the pay phone, disturbing the attached flyers and posters. "My clues led us nowhere and there aren't any new leads."

Varina frowned, but Allison had turned to reattach a flyer that had come loose. Suddenly, she squealed and gestured toward the paper. "Eric, Varina! LOOK!" she exclaimed. "We DO have a new lead."

"What?" we asked.

"Check out this flyer!"

I glanced, then scowled at an advertisement announcing a quick way to lose fifty pounds. "A weight-loss ad?" I asked skeptically.

"Not THAT flyer." Allison pointed to a light yellow

paper announcing the upcoming opening of an art exhibit.

"What's the big deal?" I shrugged. "That exhibit doesn't open for another three weeks."

"Don't you get it?" Allison asked, looking from Varina to me with excitement. "This is the La Brenz Art Gallery."

I didn't get it, but Varina's face lit up. "LA BRENZ! That's the art gallery Mrs. Carrouthers mentioned. The one Geneva Victor is sponsoring."

"Exactly," Allison said proudly. "And it's only a few blocks away."

"So what are we waiting for?" Varina asked. "Let's go."

I opened my mouth to say I just wanted to get on a plane and head home, that I was sick and tired of wild Victor chases, but before I got a chance a shrill ringing came from Varina's purse.

"My cell phone," Varina explained, reaching for the phone and flipping it open. Then she gave a soft cry of delight and declared, "It's Chase!"

THIRTY

Los Angeles, CA

Serena found it hard to believe that Chase could lip-read from so far away, and even harder to believe that Slam wanted to kill her. But when Chase repeated more of Slam's words, including the mention of a "coffin on a roof," Serena became afraid.

Chase had NO way of knowing about the coffin on the roof, she reasoned, unless he was telling the truth. It suddenly made sense. Slam had been on the roof because he was an accomplice in Ravage's death!

"You've got to get away from here," Chase told her, his gaze on the two men, who continued to talk. "There isn't much time."

"But—but I can't leave. . . . Slam was going to give me my big chance at stardom—"

"He was lying. He wants you dead because of something you know—something he doesn't want you talking about."

"The coffin. I saw the body," she said grimly.

"A dead body?" Chase gave her a puzzled look, then he was holding her hand and pulling her toward a side door. "Come on. You can tell me about it once we're on the road."

Serena glanced over at Slam, watching his expression darken as he spoke to the long-haired man. Neither man smiled and their body language was intense. She realized Chase was right. She REALLY was in trouble—more trouble than ever before.

Still, she wasn't ready to trust Chase—a total stranger—with her life.

"Why do you want to help me?" she asked him.

"Do I need a reason?"

"Duh?" Serena rolled her eyes, like this guy didn't have a clue about real life. "No one does anything without a reason."

"Maybe I'm different." His mouth set in a tense line, and he glanced away as if his thoughts made him uneasy. "Let's just go."

"Where?" With one last fearful glance at Slam, she followed Chase through a side door out of the coffee shop.

"Your family or friends. Somewhere safe."

"I don't have family and I thought Slam was my friend." Never show pain, she told herself, fighting the tears in her eyes. Just keep moving.

"I need my stuff before I go anywhere," she said to Chase, turning for a bank of elevators and pushing her floor number.

"Okay. But hurry." Chase reached in his pocket and

pulled out a cell phone. "While you're packing, I'll call some friends. They'll help you."

Serena started to ask why his friends would want to help her, but she found herself too scared to speak, so she just nodded.

The elevator dinged its arrival. And minutes later, they were inside Serena's room, shoving clothes, wigs, makeup, CDs, and more into a worn cloth-flowered suitcase.

Luckily, Amishka was still sleeping. She seldom got up before noon. Bye, Mish, Serena thought with a twinge of sadness. You really ticked me off sometimes, but you were my only friend and I'll miss you.

After they left the room and the elevator reached the lobby, the door opened, and suddenly Serena was staring into the surprised face of Slam.

"Serena?" the lead singer asked, astonished, looking from her to Chase to the suitcase. "What's going on?"

"Nothing!" she snapped, then met Chase's alert expression. Before Slam could react, they bolted sideways, Chase holding the suitcase in one hand and gripping Serena's hand in his other.

"My truck's out this way!" Chase said. "HURRY!"

They dodged groups of people, piles of suitcases, and startled employees until they reached double glass doors that led out to a side parking lot.

Serena was running fast, keeping up with Chase; excited, terrified, and yet barely out of breath. The same lungs that could belt out the highest note and hold it for an eternity gave her the stamina to keep moving.

"The red truck!" Chase shouted, pointing and sprinting around parked vehicles. He dug into his pocket and pulled out a key ring.

Serena bolted for the small red truck with a camper

shell and hurried to the passenger door. Chase unlocked his door, jumped inside, and reached over to let her in.

As she hopped onto leather cushions, she glanced behind and saw Slam and the long-haired guy running toward them. What was that dark object in Slam's hand? A GUN?

"THEY'RE AFTER US!" Serena screamed, gripping the dash in front of her. "HURRY!"

"I AM!" Chase hollered back, whipping his key into the ignition. The truck roared to life. "Hold tight!"

Then the truck burst forward, tires squealing, rubber burning, and Serena's heart thundering as she headed into an unknown future with a total stranger.

THIRTY-ONE

Varina hung up the phone, then turned to Allison and me. Her cheeks were flushed and her green eyes were bright with excitement. "That was Chase. He's found a friend of Sandee's, but there's a problem."

"What?" I asked, shifting my legs anxiously as we stood on the sidewalk.

"I don't know." Varina shrugged. "Her name is Serena and she needs some help. I told Chase we could use his help, too. So he's on his way."

"He's coming to Monterey?" Allison asked, surprised.

Varina nodded, smiling widely. "It'll take several hours, but I told him we'd have lunch and hang out at the boardwalk for a while. Then we'll meet him at the La Brenz Art Gallery."

"We're going to wait around for him?" I groaned. But when my stomach growled, I realized lunch was an excellent idea.

So we headed for the boardwalk, finding open-air food stalls that offered clam chowder, crab, shrimp, and other fishy delights. After eating at a small canopy-covered outdoor table, we wandered around the shops and the beach. Allison rolled up her jeans and boldly waded into the water, then shrieked from the coldness. I laughed and quickly ducked when she splashed water at me.

The water war lasted until we were totally soaked. Then we wandered down the beach to dry off, sitting down on a log and facing the foaming ocean.

We relaxed in silence for a while, until Allison nudged me and whispered, "Check out Varina's dopey expression."

"Huh?"

"She's thinking about Chase. I'm sure of it."

"So now you're a mind reader?" I teased.

"Nope. Just a girl." She laughed softly. "And believe me, Varina has it BAD for Chase. I only hope he feels the same way."

"Doesn't he?"

"Who knows? With Chase, it's hard to tell."

I nodded, pretending to understand. But when it came to romance, I was clueless. I'd liked a few girls at school and some had even liked me back, but I usually messed things up by clowning around or saying something lame.

The lulling sound of surf smoothed away my worries and my eyes closed. It was SO relaxing here. . . .

Time slipped away, and suddenly Allison was tapping my shoulder, startling me awake.

"We should head for the museum now," Allison said.

"Yeah." Varina glanced at her watch. "Chase will meet us within the hour. And it'll take us about thirty minutes to walk there."

"Okay," I muttered, yawning and stretching as I stood up. With one last look at the blissful blue-green Pacific Ocean, I headed up the wooden shore steps toward the street.

The La Brenz Art Gallery proved hard to find. We made four wrong turns before stumbling onto the gray rambling two-story building on a dead-end street. Even then we weren't sure we had the right place. No sign or bold lettering proclaimed that this was an art gallery. The only identifying mark was a small street address by the door.

"This has to be it," Allison said, checking the map she'd purchased at the boardwalk. "But it looks SO deserted."

"A dead building on a dead-end street," Varina said ominously.

"No cars out in front," I noticed, pushing my glasses higher on my nose. "And no lights either. What's the plan?"

"Search the place." Allison tilted her head toward me. "You ready to go inside, Eric?"

"Sure," I said, sounding braver than I felt.

"We should wait for Chase," Varina said.

"No reason to," Allison replied. "The place is deserted, so there's no danger. You can wait out here for him, then join us inside when he shows up."

Varina looked uneasy, but she agreed anyway, and Allison and I headed toward the building.

"The upstairs window on the right side is partially open," Allison pointed out. "I can boost you into it, then I'll pull myself up behind you."

I nodded, knowing she could lift much more than my weight with her super strength.

"My vision does pretty well in the dark," I said, glad

to have some super skills of my own. "Once we're inside, just follow me."

"You got it," Allison said excitedly, as if this were one of the boardwalk's thrill rides.

I glanced back and saw Varina standing in the shadows of the building across the street. She waved and gave us a thumbs-up gesture.

Then I moved toward the side of the large gray building, stepping carefully over littered garbage and uneven ground. I stopped underneath the half-opened window. It was at least four feet above my head. But when Allison bent down to lift me by the ankles, she easily boosted me way up over her head. Reaching with extended arms, I grabbed the window ledge, then pulled myself inside.

YES!! I'd made it! And with a powerful leap, Allison joined me. We were both IN!

I leaned out the window to wave at Varina, only when I glanced down, I saw something alarming.

A car was pulling up—a beige sedan driven by a petite, dark-haired woman.

I recognized her immediately.

Geneva Victor had arrived.

THIRTY-TWO

Leaving Los Angeles, CA

Serena leaned back against the car's seat and snuck a
curious look at Chase. His mouth was set in a grim
line, and his gray-blue eyes focused on the road ahead.

"Where are we going?" she asked quietly, not really
caring, just grateful to be alive.

"Monterey."

"Is that where your friends are?"

"Yeah. For today anyway." He continued to grip the
wheel tightly, with control and purpose.

"Why do we have to go to these friends? I'd rather
just stay with you."

"No you wouldn't." He glanced at her, frowning
deeply. "I have some heavy issues to figure out."

"You're being very mysterious," she said with a slow,

seductive smile. "I like that in a guy. Tell me about yourself."

"Not much to tell." He shrugged. "I used to live in Reno, only I don't anymore. I used to have two great parents, only I don't anymore. I like rock climbing and Chinese food, and I hate questions."

Now she was more intrigued than ever. And she couldn't stop staring at his rough, chiseled features. She resisted the urge to trace her finger along his cheekbones, nose, and jawline. Instead, she clasped her hands together in her lap and said, "I don't like questions either. Still, I should explain why those guys were after me."

"Something about a coffin?"

"Yeah. You probably won't believe this, but I saw a coffin with a body inside. The dead guy was Ravage."

"THE Ravage?" he asked.

"Yeah. THE Ravage. And it gets worse." Serena went on to tell the whole story.

When she'd finished, Chase nodded. "So the fake Ravage and Slam are in on the cover-up. No wonder they want you dead. If you talked to the press, they could check fingerprints and find out the truth."

"But I'm not a snitch," Serena said with a sad sigh. "And I really didn't know what to make of the whole thing. I was really too confused to go to the police."

In a softer tone that made Serena's heart jump, Chase said, "Don't worry, I'll help you out. I'm not like Slam. I promise I won't let you down."

"Thanks. That means a lot to me."

She debated about telling Chase the truth. She owed him big-time for saving her life, and yet she'd continued to lie. It wasn't right to let him search for Sandee Yoon when he'd already found her.

And yet if Chase knew that she was only fifteen and a runaway, she'd never have a chance with him. She could sense his growing interest: the way he looked at her, the gentle touch of his hand, his sincere tone.

But would he be attracted to small-town Sandee Yoon?

Nope. Not a chance.

Serena sighed.

Miles passed and she continued to struggle between truth and lies. Chase didn't say much, mostly driving in silence. Serena's head ached and she shut her eyes for a while.

When she awoke, Chase announced that they had reached Monterey.

No more time for debating. Once they met up with Chase's friends, Serena wouldn't be able to talk privately with him. Whatever his reasons for wanting to find Sandee, he deserved the truth.

"Chase, I have to tell you something," Serena began, twisting her fingers together and taking a deep breath.

"Sure." He slowed for a stop sign. "What?"

"It's important." Another deep breath. "I—I haven't been honest."

"You didn't really see a coffin?"

"No, that was the truth. This is something else—"

"There's our turnoff!" Chase pointed at a street sign, then made a sharp right that jostled Serena against the door. "Sorry. You were saying?"

She hesitated, fear seizing her words. Then she shrugged. "It can wait till we get wherever we're going."

He didn't reply, turning his attention to a map and street signs. It was nearly twenty minutes before he finally found the street he was looking for.

"That two-story warehouse must be the place," he murmured, tossing the map aside.

"Are you sure?" Serena asked. "It's SO empty-looking. There's only one car parked there."

Chase pulled up behind the parked car and shut off his engine. He lifted his head suddenly, as if he'd heard a noise. And then he turned to look at someone heading toward him.

"VARINA!" Chase exclaimed with a huge grin. He flung open his door and ran over to a girl with reddish hair.

Serena sat quietly, watching as the girl squealed with joy and wrapped her arms around Chase. She hugged him tight—way TOO tight, in Serena's opinion.

"Oh, Chase!" Varina cried. "I'm so glad you're here! I missed you SO much, and now something terrible's happened."

Serena tensed, Varina's words replaying in her mind: "I've missed you SO much." Was she Chase's girl-friend?

"Are you okay?" Chase asked Varina, holding her close and touching her hair in a gentle, familiar way. "What's happened?"

"Geneva Victor is HERE!" Varina exclaimed. "And Allison and Eric are inside with her. We've got to help them!"

Chase hurried with Varina toward the building, not even turning back to look at Serena.

Jealously flamed in her. Chase had completely for-gotten her. He'd promised she could count on him and now he was rushing off with another girl. He'd lied! She couldn't count on him—or anyone—only herself.

Well, Chase was going to be REAL sorry, she vowed.

He could have his precious Varina, but he'd never find Sandee. Serena wasn't going to wait around for a jerk she couldn't trust.

She was out of here.

THIRTY-THREE

"Eric, do you know that woman?" Allison asked me, pointing out the window.

I nodded grimly. "Geneva Victor."

"That's HER? But she looks SO harmless. Like a nice librarian or kindergarten teacher. I've never seen her close up. I imagined her with devil eyes and a witchy scowl."

"Don't let her fool you. Inside she's pure witch. All we are to her is a means to more money." I reached for Allison's hand and pulled her away from the window. "Come on, we'd better get moving."

"Yeah," she said with a solemn nod. And I was surprised to find her hands sweaty and her pulse racing. Could Allison actually be afraid? She usually seemed so strong and confident—perhaps it was all an act.

We left the small upstairs room and tiptoed to the staircase. There the strong smell of oil paints and turpentine hung in the air, and dozens of vivid seascape paintings leaned against walls.

"Should I use my vision to check things out?" I whispered to Allison.

"Go for it," she encouraged.

I handed my glasses to her and put my hands against the wall to steady myself. I immediately felt dizzy and saw blurred swirling images. My legs swayed and I'm sure I would have toppled down the staircase if Allison hadn't held me secure with her strong hands.

"You okay?" I heard her ask, only I couldn't answer. I concentrated hard on the floor, willing my eyes to see through wood and walls. Something was different this time. Luminous colors swirled and confused my vision. It was like looking through a kaleidoscope, with fragments of blues, greens, oranges, yellows, and reds twisted and tangled together.

What was happening?

The more I struggled to see beyond solid walls, the more the colors assaulted my senses. And the stench of turpentine intensified, making me nauseous and weak.

"Not . . . working," I moaned. "My . . . my glasses." I unclenched my fingers and reached out for Allison. "Give . . . me . . . glasses."

I felt Allison's fingers on my face and then the cool metal of my glasses. Taking a deep breath, I closed my eyes and then slowly opened them. Allison's concerned face swam into view, and I let out a relieved sigh. I was okay again.

"What happened?" Allison asked.

"I don't know." I rubbed my eyes. "It's never hit me like that before. I couldn't see past the bright colors, and the smell of turpentine almost choked me."

"Maybe the colors you saw were from paintings." Allison gestured to the stacks of art around us.

"Could be. But it's weird. I mean, I can see through a solid metal cabinet, but not through oil paint."

"All of the clone powers are weird: my strength, Varina's memory, Chase's hearing, and your eyesight."

"I wonder if Sandee Yoon has a power."

"Probably. But if Chase doesn't find her, we may never know." Allison headed for the staircase, glancing back and putting her finger to her lips. "Let's get moving. If we're careful, we can check out the rooms without Geneva finding us."

I nodded, moving cautiously down the staircase. The smell of turpentine grew stronger, but it didn't bother me anymore.

"Geneva alert!" I grabbed Allison's shoulder and pointed to the long hallway off the main room.

"I see her," Allison said in a frightened whisper. "And she's carrying a briefcase."

"Let's follow her." I moved forward, taking the lead.

Allison and I crept across the main room, pressed up against a wall, then peeked down the hallway just in time to see Geneva disappear into a side room.

"Come on," I mouthed. My heart was thundering, but some inner strength urged me forward.

She nodded. "I'm with you."

We crept down the hall, not making a sound. When we reached the room at the end, we came to a dead stop. A heavy, metal door barred the way.

Allison could easily break through it, I knew. But would that be a good idea? We had no idea what dangers lurked inside. What if Mitch was also there? And what if he had a gun? Rushing in blindly would be risky, unless . . .

I gulped and handed my glasses to Allison. "Hold these."

"Eric. No!" she cried softly. "You nearly passed out last time. Let's leave and get help."

But I was already focusing on the door. There was some dizziness, but it passed quickly. The gray metal faded, and then I was seeing inside the room—watching Geneva stand beside a table covered with boxes, jars, test tubes, knives, and needles, then reach out to grab a scalpel.

My heart pounded so loudly, I was sure Geneva could hear it. But she didn't turn toward the door. Her attention was on a far corner of the room, to a table draped with a white sheet. No, not just a white sheet. There was a person UNDER the sheet.

MY SISTER.

I slapped my hand over my mouth so I wouldn't gasp. Every cell in my body screamed a warning.

Allison was pulling my arm, holding me back. "What is it, Eric? What do you see?"

"Kristyn," I uttered hoarsely. If I'd had Allison's strength, nothing could have stopped me from ripping the door away. But I froze, uncertain what to do, chilled as I watched my darkest nightmare become reality.

Geneva was moving her lips, speaking to Kristyn or perhaps to herself. I couldn't hear. But I could see that Kristyn wasn't answering. Her face was pale and still, her eyes closed, and one hand hung limply over the side of the table.

No . . . she couldn't . . . she couldn't be . . .

Then I saw the faint rise of her chest beneath the white sheet, and I breathed a sigh of relief. Alive! Thank God!

But what were those scars on her upper arm? And

why was there a bandage on the side of her neck? What had Geneva done to my sister?

"Eric," Allison was whispering. "Do you want me to smash the door open? Tell me, what should we do!"

I shook my head, watching in terror as Geneva came toward Kristyn with the sharp scalpel. I had to act—FAST!

When I turned to tell Allison, my vision wouldn't focus on her. Instead it shot past walls and back into the main room of the house, where I was startled to see someone I knew.

Chase! He was here, just a few rooms away. Only he wasn't alone. The door had opened behind him, and a thin, red-haired man was peeking inside. It was Mitch! And he had a heavy pipe in his hands. Now he was lifting the pipe and moving menacingly toward Chase. . . .

I swiveled back and saw Geneva bending over my sister, the scalpel clasped purposefully in her hand. . . .

Chase!

Kristyn!

How could I save them both?

THIRTY-FOUR

"What is it, Eric?" Allison was asking. "What do you see?"

I shook my head, turning back to watch Mitch, who was now only a few feet away from Chase. Then I noticed something else. Chase was tilting his head, like he did when he used his super hearing. Did that mean he was listening to US?

"Chase!" I whispered. "I hope you can hear me because you're in BIG trouble. Mitch is behind you! DUCK!"

"Mitch? He's after Chase?" Allison gasped.

I watched Chase's expression grow alert, and just as Mitch reached out with the pipe, Chase spun around, grabbed the weapon, and lunged at Mitch.

I quickly shoved my glasses back on. "Knock down this door, Allison! Kristyn's in trouble!"

Allison didn't hesitate. She gave the door a solid push,

and it fell open as if it were a flimsy cobweb. Then she turned and raced to help Chase.

I faced Geneva—who was touching the scalpel to my sister's upper arm. The sharp blade sliced, drawing blood. . . .

"NOOOOO!" I roared with rage so powerful, I barely realized I was charging forward, kicking up at Geneva's outstretched hand, knocking the scalpel from her fingers so that it soared away and then clattered to the floor.

Geneva gave a frightened scream and backed away. "Who—what?" she sputtered.

"Stay away from my sister!" I hollered, fueled by vengeance. I wasn't thinking, only moving toward Geneva, wanting her to suffer. . . .

"Eric?" a voice said weakly. "Is . . . is it you?"

I stopped instantly and turned to see Kristyn's eyes fluttering open. The cut on her arm oozed blood and tears trickled down her cheeks.

"Kristyn!" I cried as I flew to her side, forgetting about Geneva, who scrambled away from me. "Are you all right?"

"Eric?" She moaned and shook her tousled black hair. "I . . . I hurt."

"Oh, Kris. I'm so sorry." I found some tissues and a bandage and covered Kristyn's cut. Then I hugged her, so relieved that she was safe.

I felt sick with guilt, especially when I saw the needle marks and scars on Kristyn's arm and neck. What had she endured? I couldn't even imagine . . . and I was afraid to. This was all my fault.

There were loud footsteps, and then Chase appeared in the doorway. Beside him stood Varina. They were both smiling.

"Allison is tying Mitch up," Chase said, wiping a blob

of blue paint from his face. "That creep won't give us any more trouble."

"What did you do?" I held tight to Kristyn's frail hand.

"I knocked him down, but it was Varina who burst in and nailed him with a jar of blue paint."

"Who knew paint could be so dangerous?" Varina flashed a warm, proud smile. "I'm just glad you're okay."

I suddenly looked around, realizing that someone was missing. "What about Geneva? Where'd she go?"

Chase shrugged. "I didn't see her."

Varina pointed to a back door, which stood ajar. "She must have slipped out through there."

"Darn!" I cried. "She got away!"

"At least we got Mitch." Chase patted me on the back. "And it looks like you found your sister."

"Eric saved me," Kristyn said softly, holding the tissue over her injured arm and giving me a faint smile.

I felt a rush of pride, a sense of finally having done something right. But I shook my head. "I had help: Allison, Varina, and Chase. We did it together."

From outside I heard the whine of sirens.

"About time the police got here," Varina said. "I called them from my cell phone."

Kristyn tugged on my hand. "Eric . . . I want . . . to go . . . home."

"Soon, Kristyn," I promised. "We'll both go home."

Moments later, the police arrived, followed by reporters and ambulances. I stayed with Kristyn as she was wheeled into an ambulance, smoothing back her hair and squeezing her hand to reassure her.

While the paramedics checked out Kristyn, I heard Varina call for Chase, Allison, and me. Turning, I saw

Varina standing by Chase's red minitruck. The truck door was open, and Varina was gesturing inside.

Chase had heard Varina's call and was hurrying over. I headed over there, too.

"What's up?" I asked Varina.

"Look what I found on the car seat!" Varina held out a piece of paper to Chase. "I think it's for you."

There was a dark expression on Chase's face as he read the note. Suddenly, he balled his fist and smacked it into the palm of his other hand. "Damn! I blew it!"

"What?" I raised my brows.

"How could I have let her out of my sight?"

"Chase, what's wrong?" I asked. "Who wrote the note?"

"Read it for yourself," Chase said, controlled fury smoldering under his words.

I took the note and read:

Chase—

Thanks for getting me out of a jam. But you promised I could count on you. You LIED. And I don't hang out with liars.

Don't look for me. I'm already someone else by now—someone who doesn't want to see you EVER again.

And guess what? Serena isn't my real name. Ha! The joke's on you.

Bye . . . Sandee Yoon

"SANDEE YOON!" I exclaimed, handing the note back to Chase. "You found her? Why didn't you tell us?"

"I suspected it, but I didn't want to let her know that.

I was afraid she'd bolt if I confronted her with it." Chase shook his head and swore under his breath. Then he crumpled the note into a wrinkled, withered ball, smashed it between his palms, and threw it away.

THIRTY-FIVE

Time is a funny thing. If you're sitting in a classroom, watching the heavy hands on a clock, seconds crawl by. But when life gets crazy, throws you confusing curves, time races by without measure or meaning.

Three weeks had passed since Kristyn and I returned home. Twenty-one days that included a bittersweet Christmas, a not-so-happy New Year, and deep smoldering layers of guilt.

On the surface everything was okay. Mitch was in jail for good, charged with kidnapping and murder. He couldn't hurt anyone ever again. Geneva had been slicker, creating an alibi that fooled the police, if not us clones. She had opened her art gallery and gone on with her life.

Kristyn was safe at home, but she wasn't the same person she'd been before the kidnapping. Her external scars may have healed, but they grew deeper inside, haunting her soul. She had nightmares, was afraid to leave the house, and had started seeing a therapist.

I blamed myself.

So I began to make secret plans.

I exchanged E-mails with Allison, who at my insistence had started using her laptop. And I had many whispered phone conversations with Varina, as well as with her uncle.

Then the day came to spring the plan on my parents.

"Mom, Dad, I have something important to say," I told them, finding courage and confidence. I began by reminding my parents that Kristyn had been kidnapped because she'd been mistaken for a clone. But I was the clone, not Kristyn. So it was MY fault my sister had suffered. I couldn't change my unusual past, but I could take charge of my future.

And then I told them what I planned to do.

Naturally, they objected. But I insisted, and after a few days of heated discussions, my parents realized that the best way to protect the whole family was to let me go.

So I began packing for my new life in California.

THIRTY-SIX

W ell, I'd survived my first day as a new student at the same school Varina attended, Seymore High. I'd enjoyed meeting Varina's friends, especially her outrageous friend Starr—now that was one COOL girl. Sure, I missed my family, but life here was definitely interesting.

Varina's uncle, Jim Fergus, had officially opened a boarding and tutoring service for "gifted students." So far there were just three students: Varina, Allison, and me. Chase had left again . . . back searching for Sandee. Since finding her note, his moods had been darker than ever. I hoped he'd find her soon.

After school, Varina, Allison, and I walked home together, talking about normal stuff like teachers and homework. We were fast becoming a family, or "clone cousins," as Allison still liked to call us. Soon we'd be staying at a new, larger home. Varina's uncle was making plans to move to a bigger house, and the new place would have a cutting-edge security system, which would make us all rest easier.

As Varina, Allison, and I walked up to the house, I sensed that something was up when Varina whispered to Allison. Allison whispered back, glancing over at me. Then they both giggled.

"What's going on?" I asked suspiciously.

"You'll find out."

I gave them a deep stare, more suspicious than ever. Then they giggled again and raced into the house.

Frowning, I followed. I reached the front door and opened it cautiously. There was a startling, sharp sound. Then suddenly a large golden whirl of fur bounded toward me, barking joyfully, knocking me backward, and landing on my chest. A sloppy red tongue began licking my face.

"RENEGADE!" I shouted happily. I couldn't believe it!

Allison and Varina shouted, "Surprise!"

I hugged my dog some more, happier than I'd been in weeks. "Thanks! This is the BEST surprise ever!"

"I knew you'd love it," Varina said.

"It was MY idea," Allison added proudly.

Varina's uncle Jim stepped into the living room, leaning heavily on his cane. A smile peeked out through his bristling salt-and-pepper beard. "It'll be good to have a dog around the house," he said. "He's a great dog, Eric."

"And you guys are great, too." I hugged my dog, feeling a connection to my old life. Then I looked around. "Hey, I need a ball. Renegade plays a mean game of catch."

"We should have a tennis ball around here somewhere," Uncle Jim said.

"I think I saw one in the hall closet," Allison said.

I followed Allison through the hall, then idly reached down to scratch Renegade's head as I waited for her. I heard her mumble, "Found it . . . Hmmm . . . What's this?"

She tossed me a ball, then eased out of the closet, holding an old magazine in her hands. There was a strange expression on her face.

"You okay, Al?" I asked, throwing the ball a short way down the hall so Renegade could scramble after it.

"I'm not sure. . . ." Allison kept staring at the magazine. Her mouth fell open, and she gave an excited gasp. "Eric! LOOK!"

"Why?" I shrugged. "It's just an old magazine."

"NO!" She shook her head. "It's much more! Don't you see?"

All I saw was a fashion magazine, dated nearly twenty years ago, with a slim blond model on the cover wearing a skimpy swimming suit. Then I noticed something else.

"WOW!" I gave a low whistle. "Allison, the model looks like YOU."

"Exactly like me. Her long blond hair, brown eyes, wide mouth, and even the cluster of freckles on her thigh are like mine."

"What a cool coincidence."

"NO! It's not a coincidence. It's much more. She doesn't JUST look like me. She IS me. Or maybe I'm her." Allison's eyes grew wide and astonished. "I'm her clone."

ABOUT THE AUTHOR

Linda Joy Singleton lives on three acres near Sacramento, California, with her supportive husband, David, and two terrific teens, Melissa and Andy. She has a barnyard of animals, including horses, pigs, cats, dogs, and a goat. One of the newest dogs to her family is named Renegade.

Linda Joy Singleton is the author of over twenty juvenile novels, as well as numerous short "chiller" stories. Links to these stories and other information about the author can be found at her web site: http://www.geocities.com/Athens/Acropolis/4815/.